When Matt looked up, she offered him a shy smile. "Like I said, I'm sorry. I should have told you about Emily."

"You've got that right."

"I've made mistakes, but Emily isn't one of them. She's a great kid. So for now, let's focus on her."

"All right." Matt uncrossed his arms and raked a hand through his hair. "But just for the record, I would've done anything in my power to take care of you and Emily."

"I know." And that was why she'd walked away from him. Matt would have stood up to her father, challenged his threat, only to be knocked to his knees—and worse.

No, leaving town and cutting all ties with Matt was the only thing she could've done to protect him.

As she stood in the room where their daughter was conceived, as she studied the only man she'd ever loved, the memories crept up on her, the old feelings, too.

Once upon a time, there'd been something about the fun-loving nineteen-year-old cowboy that had drawn her attention when she'd been sixteen. And whatever it was continued to tug at her now.

* * *

ROCKING CHAIR RODEO:
Cowboys—and true love—never go out of style!

Dear Reader,

Honey, my fur grandbaby, is the inspiration for the dog in this book. And like Sweetie Pie, the fictitious shepherd mix, Honey is a slow learner and hell-bent on catching the neighborhood skunk. She also likes to chase any delivery drivers who dare to bring mail or packages to her house. As a result, she has landed on the UPS, FedEx and USPS naughty lists.

But it's not just the critters that are appealing in this story. *The Cowboy's Secret Family* has all of my favorite ingredients for a romance—first love, a secret baby, a pregnant runaway bride and, of course, a handsome rodeo cowboy.

You first met Matt Grimes in *The Soldier's Twin Surprise* (Harlequin Special Edition, July 2018). Now it's Matt's turn to have his story told.

After suffering a career-threatening injury while bull riding, Matt returns home to his uncle's ranch to recuperate, only to find Miranda Contreras has temporarily moved in with her eight-year-old daughter and an ever-increasing barnyard menagerie. Miranda broke Matt's heart nine years ago when she left town, deserting him without saying goodbye. Now she's back, pregnant with another man's baby, yet more stunning and attractive than ever.

I hope you'll enjoy Matt and Miranda's story as much as I enjoyed writing it. Wishing you romance!

Judy

PS: I love hearing from my readers. You can contact me through my website, judyduarte.com. You can also contact me on Facebook at Facebook.com/judyduartenovelist.

The Cowboy's
Secret Family

———

Judy Duarte

HARLEQUIN® SPECIAL EDITION

Recycling programs
for this product may
not exist in your area.

ISBN-13: 978-1-335-57390-2

The Cowboy's Secret Family

Copyright © 2019 by Judy Duarte

Printed in U.S.A.

Since 2002, *USA TODAY* bestselling author **Judy Duarte** has written over forty books for Harlequin Special Edition, earned two RITA® Award nominations, won two Maggie Awards and received a National Readers' Choice Award. When she's not cooped up in her writing cave, she enjoys traveling with her husband and spending quality time with her grandchildren. You can learn more about Judy and her books on her website, judyduarte.com, or at Facebook.com/judyduartenovelist.

Books by Judy Duarte

Harlequin Special Edition

Rocking Chair Rodeo

Roping in the Cowgirl
The Bronc Rider's Baby
A Cowboy Family Christmas
The Soldier's Twin Surprise
The Lawman's Convenient Family

The Fortunes of Texas: All Fortune's Children

Wed by Fortune

The Fortunes of Texas: The Secret Fortunes

From Fortune to Family Man

The Fortunes of Texas: The Rulebreakers

No Ordinary Fortune

Visit the Author Profile page
at Harlequin.com for more titles.

To "Honey" Colwell,
my fur grandchild and the inspiration for
Sweetie Pie, the rescued stray dog in
The Cowboy's Secret Family. No matter how many
times Honey gets sprayed by Eau de Stink,
she's determined to catch the rascally skunk
that prowls the neighborhood at night.
Maybe next time, Honey.

And to Jeff and Sarah Colwell.
Thank you for the opportunity to spend a
special summer with Emalee and Katie, my
two granddaughters, and a barnyard menagerie
consisting of one overly protective shepherd mix,
six free-range chickens, two 4-H lambs and a
couple of horses. Love you, guys!

Chapter One

The new Dodge Ram pickup bounced along the graveled drive that led to the Double G Ranch, where Matt Grimes intended to hole up until he recovered from his injury and could return to the rodeo circuit.

The afternoon sun's glare was damn near blinding, so he reached for the visor, only to miss spotting another pothole, this one bigger than the last. Pain shot through his bum knee, and he swore under his breath. He'd have to convince Uncle George that it was finally time to pave the blasted road or they'd need an all-terrain vehicle to get to the house.

Matt hadn't been home since the Christmas before last, so he probably should have called to let his uncle know he was coming, but he'd decided to surprise him.

He swerved to avoid another hole, a quick move that

jarred his knee again, and he gritted his teeth in pain. The last bull he'd ridden, Grave Digger, had thrown him to the ground, stepping on him in the process. He hadn't suffered a fracture, only tissue damage. But it hurt like hell, and the doctor seemed to think it would take a while for him to heal.

But come hell or high water, Matt was determined to compete in the Rocking Chair Rodeo, which would benefit two of his favorite charities—a local home for retired cowboys, as well as one for abused and neglected kids. On top of that, Esteban Enterprises had used Matt's name to promote the rodeo, and all the ads and posters sported his photo and practically claimed *Local Boy Makes Good.* Hopefully, he'd heal quickly so he could live up to the hype.

When he pulled up to the small ranch house and parked, he remained behind the wheel for a while, rubbing the ache in his knee and stunned as he scanned the yard and noticed how different things were. Damn. His uncle had been busy. No wonder he hadn't gotten around to fixing the road yet.

A lamb stood under a canopy covering part of a small pen near the barn. A new chicken coop had been built, too, with several hens clucking and pecking at the ground. A black-and-white Shetland pony was corralled near the house and an unfamiliar car was parked in the drive.

What in the hell was going on? Had Uncle George hired someone new? He had ranch hands who worked the cattle, but he'd never put a lot of effort into the yard.

Matt climbed out of the truck, wincing when he

put weight on his right leg. As he reached for his cane, a mixed-breed dog wearing a red Western kerchief around its neck rushed at him, barking as if it had super-canine strength and planned to take on a pack of wolves.

Before Matt had to fend off the shepherd-mix with his cane, Uncle George stepped out onto the porch from inside the house, squinting at the glare caused by the sunlight hitting a metal wind chime—a fancy addition that hadn't been there before.

George lifted his hand to shade his eyes and called off the stupid mutt. It obeyed the old man's gruff tone, but it still eyed Matt as if it wasn't yet convinced he wasn't a burglar who'd come to rob the ranch at gunpoint.

"What's going on?" Matt asked, his voice edged with irritation.

The screen door screeched open again, and out walked a little girl in pigtails wearing a white blouse with a green 4-H kerchief tied around her neck, blue jeans and sneakers. The dog took a look at her, wagged its tail and then began barking at Matt all over again.

The girl hurried to the mutt, dropped to her knees and hugged the dog's neck. "Shush, Sweetie Pie. It's okay."

"Well, look what the cat dragged in," Uncle George finally said. "My long-lost nephew. What'd you do? Lose your cell phone?"

"I've been busy." While that was true, Matt still should have called. Maybe then he'd know who that little girl was. Had his uncle taken on a babysitting gig to supplement his Social Security? And what was with the menagerie—ponies, chickens, dogs and who knew what else?

A soft breeze kicked up, causing the wind chime to tinkle, while Matt tried to make sense of it all. Before he could prod his uncle for an explanation, the girl turned to the house and called out, "Mommy! Hurry up. We're going to be late to the 4-H meeting."

Matt leaned on his cane, confused. Dazed. He shot a glance at his uncle. The white-haired man still favored jeans and flannel shirts, like the red one he wore today. His clothes fit him much better. The tall, lanky man had filled out since the last time Matt had been home.

Apparently, "Mommy" was a good cook.

As Matt took a step toward his uncle, his bad knee nearly gave out, causing him to wince and wobble. He used his cane for balance and swore under his breath.

"You'd better sit down before you fall down," George said. "What'd you do to yourself?"

"Crossed paths with the wrong bull." Matt hobbled up the steps to the wraparound porch, which was adorned with pots of red geraniums and colorful pansies. He had no idea how long "Mommy" had been here, but long enough to make her mark.

"One day a bull is gonna break your neck instead of your leg," Uncle George said. "I hope you learned your lesson this time and are finally giving up the rodeo. You're getting too old for that crazy kid stuff."

"It's barely a scratch. I'll be ready to ride again—or even have another run-in with Grave Digger—in a few weeks." Matt glanced at the colorful heart-shaped wel-come mat at the door. "Is my room available?"

His uncle gestured to one of the rockers on the porch. "Your room is always ready for you. I keep thinking you'll finally come to your senses and move home where you belong."

Matt limped to a chair. He didn't really *belong* any-where, a lesson he'd learned early on. He took a seat, rested his cane against the small wicker table and set his rocker in motion. His uncle sat in the chair next to his.

For a moment, he savored the familiar earthy scent of the only place that came close to being the home he could actually call his own. But now he wasn't so sure about that. Apparently, a lot had changed in the past year and a half.

Matt lowered his voice and asked, "So what's going on?"

His uncle shrugged a single shoulder, then placed an arthritic index finger to his lips and shushed him. "Hold your questions for a while."

Matt nodded as if that made perfect sense, but noth-ing about this situation did, and his curiosity grew to the point that it was downright troublesome.

He studied the child. She was a cute little thing. He guessed her to be about six or seven.

She cocked her head to the side, one brown pigtail dangling over her shoulder, and eyed Matt carefully. "Who are *you*?"

He could ask her the same thing, but he supposed

he'd have wait until after she and her mother left to have the bulk of his questions answered.

"I'm Matt," he said.

"Oh." She nodded, her pigtails swishing up and down. "You're the cowboy who used to live here. That's what I thought. I'm Emily. Me and my mom are staying here. We'll probably go home someday, but I hope we don't. I like having a big yard."

So Emily and "Mommy" lived in a town. Or in a city.

The screen door squeaked open once again and a twenty-something brunette stepped onto the porch. She shielded her eyes from the sun's glare off the metal chimes with her hand, blocking her face, but recognition slammed into Matt like a bull out of the shoot.

Miranda Contreras.

His old teenage crush. The girl who'd strung him along before breaking his heart beyond repair. And here she was again, all grown up, prettier than ever and rocking Matt's world again, just as she'd done the day she arrived at Wexler High, a pretty sophomore with a bubbly laugh.

She stepped out of the sunlight's glare, and when her eyes met his, she flinched. Her lips parted and she placed a hand on her chest as if she hadn't expected to see him ever again. *"Matt?"*

"Miranda." His body tensed, and he kept his tone cool. But inside his gut coiled into a knot.

She swept a glossy strand of dark hair behind her ear. A nervous gesture?

"It's been a long time," she said.

"Yep." Too long, it seemed. But maybe not long enough.

Matt's gaze swept across the yard, from the pony in the corral, to the chickens in the coop, to the lamb in the pen and then to the little brown-haired girl hugging the dog.

Was Miranda responsible for all of...*this*?

She had to be.

But why in the hell, after all these years, had she come back to the Double G? And how long did she intend to stay?

Uncle George had made it clear that he ought to hold his questions until after they left, but the curiosity was eating him alive.

"I see a pony in the corral," Matt said to the child. "Did you bring it with you when you came to the Double G?"

"No, she's brand-new. I mean, she's not a baby. She's just a little horse. And she's already grown up. Uncle George gave her to me because I'm going to be a cowgirl when I grow up."

Uncle George? Back in the day, Miranda had claimed his father's uncle as her own. And now she'd encouraged her daughter do the same thing. It hadn't bothered Matt a bit when they were younger, because if things had worked out between them, that relationship might have become official. But that's not the way their teenage romance had played out.

For that reason, having Miranda here knocked his blood pressure out of whack, especially since he had the feeling she'd moved in permanently. Her daughter might think they were going back home one of these days, wherever that home was. But flowers on the porch, a pony in the corral and a dog guarding the yard suggested otherwise.

"Guess what?" Emily asked, as she placed her small hands on her denim-clad hips. "I can saddle my pony all by myself."

"Good for you." As angry as Matt might be with her mother, he couldn't fault the cute little girl with a splash of freckles across her nose. He wondered whether she favored Miranda or maybe her father, whoever he might be. It had been years since he and Miranda had split. When had she had Emily? How old was she?

Before he could ask the little girl her age, Miranda stepped off the porch, her purse slung over her shoulder. "We'll have to play catch up later, Matt. If Emily and I don't leave now, we'll be late."

Good. Uncle George had some explaining to do.

Miranda turned to the old man and blessed him with a smile. "I have a pot roast in the oven."

"Is it big enough to feed a drifter?" George asked.

She hesitated, then smiled. "Yes, of course." She turned her gaze to Matt. "There's plenty." Then she held her hand out for Emily. "Come on, honey."

Matt watched them walk toward her car. Miranda wore a loose-fitting summer dress—a soft yellow with a floral print. She looked as fresh as spring, although she'd obviously grown up—and changed. She had womanly curves now. And, if anything, she was even prettier than before.

Once she started the car and headed down the drive, Matt turned to his uncle. "Okay. What gives?"

"Miranda and Emily needed a place to stay for a while, and I had plenty of room. They've been good company."

The subtext was clear. Matt hadn't been around much. He shook off a twinge of guilt, promising himself he'd have to do better from now on. Then he leaned back and set his rocker in motion again. "So what's her story?"

"She needed time to sort through some things, and we both figured this was the perfect place for her to do it."

"What'd she need to think about?"

"Back in February, she broke her engagement. I 'spect she's got a few things to sort through."

Two months ago? Damn. Each answer George provided only stirred up more questions. "What made her back out?"

"You know me. I don't like to pry."

Matt blew out a sigh. "Does Miranda's father know she's here?"

"Nope. And she doesn't want him to know."

Matt stiffened, and the rocker stalled. "Are you kidding? No one's come looking for her yet?"

"Not here. She told him she was staying with a friend, and her dad must have assumed it was someone she'd met in college. He's called her cell phone a few times, but he doesn't have any idea where she is."

"That's not good." Matt blew out a ragged sigh.

"You remember what happened the last time he found her here."

"I sure as hell haven't forgotten." George's rocker picked up speed, creaking against the wooden floor. "He got so angry and red in the face that I damn near thought he was either going to have a stroke or I'd have to shoot him full of buckshot."

Matt hadn't forgotten that day, either. Or the words Carlos Contreras had said to Miranda. *I can't believe you've been sneaking around with a good-for-nothing-wannabe cowboy who won't amount to a hill of beans.*

Matt had spent the past eight years riding his heart out—what was left of it, anyway. He'd shown the rodeo world that he was more than good enough for anyone, even Carlos Contreras's daughter. But he doubted his skill and a collection of silver buckles had done a damn thing to change the old man's opinion of him. Not that it mattered. That teen fling had ended a long time ago, validated by a phone that never rang.

"So what's the deal with Emily?"

George stopped rocking, leaned to the side and grinned. "She's a real sweetheart. Spunky, too. And she loves animals. You've met Sweetie Pie, the stray she talked me into keeping."

"Yeah, I met the dog. But that name doesn't suit a mutt who nearly chewed off my leg when I got out of my truck and started walking toward the door."

His uncle chuckled and folded his arms across his chest. "Animals love her, too. She really has a way with them, including the chickens. I can't tell those hens apart, but she can. Heck, she's named each one."

"That wasn't what I meant." Matt leaned toward his uncle and lowered his tone. "How *old* is she?"

"Seven or eight, I reckon."

A feeling of uneasiness began to niggle at Matt. Something about the timeline felt...wrong.

"Who's her father?" Matt asked, watching for the hint of a smile or a twinkle in his uncle's tired blue eyes, which seemed to be a lot livelier these days. But George had a talent for donning a good poker face when he wanted to.

"You'll have to ask Miranda," George said, the rocking chair creaking against the porch's wooden flooring.

"Didn't *you* ask?"

Uncle George shrugged and said, "You know me..."

"Right. You don't like to pry." Normally, Matt didn't, either, but that didn't mean he wouldn't do it as soon as he had the chance to get Miranda alone.

By the time Miranda drove within a mile of the Wexler Grange Hall, where the 4-H sheep group was gathering this afternoon, her nerves were still on edge and her mind scrambling to control her jumbled emotions.

When she'd come outside to tell Emily it was time to leave, she'd just about dropped to the ground when she'd spotted Matt at the Double G. Sure, she'd known that he could show up any day, but the rodeo circuit was in full swing, and George had told her that he rarely came home these days. So he was the last thing she'd expected to see this afternoon.

Hardly a day went by that she didn't think of her teenage love. The way she left. The guilt she felt. The secret she kept… She glanced in the rearview mirror at the eight-year-old secret that was sitting in the backseat right now.

But it wasn't just the negative feelings that struck her. She often thought of the good things, too.

Wherever she went, indoors or out, the memories dogged her. Riding horses out by the swimming hole. Fishing for trout with a makeshift pole. Having a picnic on the trail. Eating a bowl of ice cream with two spoons. And sharing sweet stolen kisses—here, there and everywhere.

So when she first spotted Matt, she'd assumed her mind was playing tricks on her again, just as it always did whenever she saw a shadow in the barn or heard George talking to someone only to find out it was his horse. After staying with George for the past two months, she'd begun to think Matt wouldn't come home while she and Emily were here. A champion bull rider like him would never do that while the rodeo season was in full swing.

But she'd been wrong. The minute she realized the handsome cowboy wasn't an illusion—that she was actually looking at Matt in the flesh, that she was gazing into those expressive green eyes—her heart took a flying leap, only to belly flop into her stomach, threatening to stir up the morning sickness that had stopped plaguing her six weeks ago.

Somehow, she'd managed to rally and find her voice. She just hoped it had sounded polite and unaffected.

"Mommmmy!" Emily called from the backseat, her

voice raised, her tone irritated. "I called your name *three* times. Aren't you *listening* to me?"

Obviously not. She'd been too busy daydreaming about the past... "I'm sorry, honey. I didn't mean to ignore you. What did you say?"

Emily blew out a dramatic sigh. "Can Janie come over after the meeting with us? And if her mom says it's okay, can she spend the night?"

Miranda glanced in the rearview mirror. Emily's eyes—the shape of them, not the color—were so much like Matt's that her heart squeezed. "No, honey. This isn't a good time to have a friend over."

"But it's Saturday, and we don't have school tomorrow. Why *can't* she?"

"Because we have a full house at the ranch already." And this evening, things would be awkward at best. But she wasn't about to reveal the real reason to her daughter. "Besides, Matt hasn't been home in a long time, and he's probably just passing through. So until I find out when he's leaving, I don't want to schedule a play date."

Surely, he'd be gone in the morning. Monday at the latest. But he was using a cane, so obviously he'd been injured. Had he come home to recuperate? If so, how long would that take?

Miranda broke eye contact with her daughter and studied the road ahead, watching for the entrance of the Wexler Grange Hall. But she couldn't keep her mind off Matt. He'd certainly grown up since she'd last seen him. His lanky nineteen-year-old body had filled out. His muscles were bulkier, his shoulders broader. He'd been sitting in a rocking chair on the porch, so it was hard to know for sure, but she suspected he'd grown a bit taller, too.

He wore his sandy-blond hair longer than she remembered—or maybe he just needed a haircut. Either way, she liked it.

An inch-long scar over his brow and a five o'clock shadow gave him a rugged edge, which, for some strange reason, added to the perfection of his face.

If he'd smiled or flashed his dimples, suggesting that he was glad to see her, her heart would have soared. Instead, he hadn't seemed the least bit happy that they'd crossed paths. Of course, she really couldn't blame him. She'd left him without saying goodbye, let alone offering an explanation.

She suspected he was long over her by now. She'd followed his rodeo success and heard rumors of the parade of buckle bunnies that followed him from city to city, hoping for a date—or whatever. From what she'd heard, Matt was even more footloose and reckless now than he used to be.

As she turned the car into the parking lot, a thought slammed into her like a deployed air bag, a possibility she hadn't considered.

What if his injury was permanent? What if he'd made a career change? What if he planned to stay on the Double G indefinitely? There was no way they could all live in the same house. And then there was the baby to think of...

Her first impulse was to go back to the ranch as soon as the 4-H meeting was over, pack their things and leave as quickly as possible. But she couldn't do that. Dodging uncomfortable situations had become a habit, one she was determined to break. Besides, a move like that was likely to crush her daughter.

Before shutting off the ignition, she took one last look in the rearview mirror and watched Emily wave at her friend Janie. The two girls planned to show their lambs at the county fair in a couple of weeks, and Miranda had never seen her daughter happier.

For Emily's sake, Miranda would deal with her feelings, as jumbled as they were. Besides, how hard could that be? She could handle the discomfort and awkwardness for a day or two.

But if Matt's stay stretched much longer, she'd be toast.

Chapter Two

Now that the dinner hour had arrived, and they'd gathered around the kitchen table, Matt and Miranda sat in silence. Once friends and lovers, now strangers at best.

She studied her plate, her glossy brown hair draping both sides of her face and making it difficult to read her expression. Matt bet she felt nearly as uneasy about their unexpected reunion as he did.

The past stretched between them like a frayed rubber band ready to snap. But he'd be damned if he'd be the first to speak.

"Emily," Uncle George said, "how'd your 4-H meeting go?"

"It was good. Miss Sadie, our leader, gave us the schedule for the county fair." The girl looked at Uncle

George with hopeful eyes. "You're going to come watch me, too. Right?"

"Honey," he said, "I wouldn't miss it for the world."

Matt swept his fork across his empty plate, stirring the leftover gravy. The fair was a couple of weeks away, so Miranda clearly planned to stick around for a while, and that left a bad taste in his mouth in spite of the fact that the damned meal she'd fixed tonight was delicious. He might have asked for seconds, but he wanted an excuse to leave the table.

Hell, as it was, he'd thought about going somewhere else to recover. At least until after the fair ended.

"Miranda," Uncle George said, patting his belly, "this pot roast is the best I've ever had."

She glanced up from her plate, which had held her interest for the past ten minutes, even though she hadn't taken more than a couple of bites. "Thank you. I'm glad you liked it." Then she returned her focus on her food.

Matt had planned to order plenty of meals for him and his uncle at Caroline's Diner since George's favorite kitchen appliance was a can opener. Now, he supposed, he wouldn't have to. That is, if he could deal with having Miranda around, stirring up the memories, both good and bad.

He supposed he ought to compliment her cooking and thank her, too. He might feel like shutting her out of his mind, like she'd done to him, but he hadn't forgotten his manners.

Before he could open his mouth, his uncle added, "I really lucked out when you came to visit, Miranda.

I'm eating better than ever, my check register finally balances and the ranch books are finally in order."

Matt dropped his fork on the plate. The thought of Miranda looking over the Double G's finances struck a ragged nerve—and for more reasons than one. George Grimes might be rough around the edges, but he had a soft heart, which sometimes got him into trouble when he put too much trust in the wrong person.

"You've got a good eye for detail, Miranda. You spotted things in the books that my accountant missed." George chuckled and crossed his arms. "I liked being able to point them out to him, too. I told him I had my very own CPA living right down the hall."

"I'm glad I could help," Miranda said, her voice almost too soft for Matt to hear.

Apparently, she'd become an accountant. That wasn't surprising. She'd been a good student when she'd been in high school, which was one reason her father had made such big plans for her.

So why was she here, when she could be helping her wealthy old man run one of the biggest berry farm operations in Texas?

Uncle George mentioned that she'd broken her engagement recently. Why? And who was the guy she'd planned to marry? Did he work for or with her father?

George said he hadn't quizzed her, which seemed doubtful since he'd always had a soft spot for her. He also had a way of getting people to open up and tell him things without the need to ask.

Either way, something wasn't right.

Matt glanced across the table at Emily, who was

stirring her carrots with a fork, trying to make it look like she'd actually eaten her veggies.

She was a cute kid, petite and dark-haired like her mother. He still wondered about her dad. And Matt was determined to learn more. Uncle George wasn't the only one in the family who was adept at ferreting out information indirectly.

"Emily," Matt said, first making eye contact with the girl before shifting his focus to her mother. "I think it's cool that you're in the 4-H. When I was in school, I knew a couple of kids who were in the 4-H, but they were older than you. Isn't there an age requirement?"

Miranda stiffened.

"I'm old enough," Emily said. "People sometimes think that I'm younger than I am because I'm small for my age, just like my mom. When I joined, the lady who signed me up wanted to put me in Cloverbuds, but that's for kids who are five to seven."

"So you just made it, huh?" Matt smiled at the child, then turned to her mother, whose lovely tanned complexion had paled.

"My birthday's on August third," Emily said, a grin dimpling her cheeks, her eyes bright. "I'm going to be nine."

It didn't take a CPA to do the math. Miranda left town nine years ago last October, which meant she must have been pregnant at the time. And if so, that meant... Matt's hand fisted and his eyes widened.

Emily was his.

Matt knew. And he clearly wasn't happy about the secret Miranda had kept from him.

What little dinner she'd eaten tonight churned in her stomach, swirling and rising as if it had nowhere to go but out. Thankfully, she was able to hold it down. She placed her hand on her stomach, only to feel her growing baby bump. But this was one bout of nausea she couldn't blame on pregnancy. Her morning sickness had passed more than a month ago.

The frown on Matt's face and the crease in his brow suggested it was taking every bit of his self-control not to...

Not to *what*? Throw something across the room like Gavin once did when he'd come across a mess Emily had left in his family room?

This time, it was Miranda who'd made a complete mess of things. But Matt wasn't like the man she'd nearly married, the marital bullet she'd dodged.

At least he hadn't been like that in the past.

"Guess what." Emily speared a potato, but rather than lifting her fork, she smiled and directed her words at Matt. "Uncle George said I could have my birthday party here."

"He did, huh?" Matt's demeanor, so stiff and strained moments ago, seemed to soften ever so slightly. His expression did, too, although it was unreadable. "Is your dad coming?"

Miranda's lips parted. She wanted to respond for the child, but the words wouldn't form. The time had come to tell Emily about Matt and vice versa, but Miranda wasn't sure what to say in front of an audience. Especially this one.

"No, he can't. Because my dad died when I was a baby."

Matt shot a fiery look at Miranda. He didn't say a word, but he didn't have to. She saw the anger, the pain, the accusation in his eyes.

She wanted to defend herself, to tell him that Emily hadn't gotten that idea from her. She must have come to that conclusion on her own. Instead, she watched as Matt got to his feet, wincing as he reached first for his cane with one hand, then stacked his glass and silverware on his empty plate with the other.

As he started for the sink, Miranda pushed her chair away from the table and stood. "Don't worry about clearing the table or doing the dishes."

He glanced over his shoulder, his glare enough to weld her to the floor, the silent accusation enough to suck the air out of the room.

"I'll explain later," she said, her voice soft, wounded.

"Don't bother." He rinsed his plate and placed it in the sink. Then he left the kitchen, his cane tapping out his anger, disappointment and who knew what else in some kind of weird Morse code.

This was *so* not the way she'd intended to tell him,

She stole a peek at George, his craggy brow furrowed, his tired blue eyes fixed on Emily. She knew that the sweet but crotchety old man had put two and two together the minute he spotted Miranda and Emily standing on his front porch. He hadn't asked any questions or judged her. He'd merely stepped aside and welcomed her, his so-called niece, and her daughter into his cluttered but cozy home. Then he'd done his best to make them feel comfortable and told them they could stay as long as they wanted.

God bless that man to the moon and back.

"Emily." Miranda sucked in a deep fortifying breath, held it for a beat, then slowly and quietly let it out. "What makes you think your daddy died?"

Emily bit down on her bottom lip and scrunched her brow as if struggling with the answer. Finally, she lowered her voice and sheepishly said, "*Abuelito* told me."

Miranda winced. Her father had overstepped once again, although he hadn't done so in years. Not since Emily was a baby and Miranda had finally put him in his place. Or so she'd thought.

"Honey," Miranda said, "if you had questions about your father, you should have asked me."

"I would have, but *Abuelito* said you didn't like to talk about my father because it made you sad. So it was better if we forgot about him." Emily glanced down at her half-eaten meal, her long pigtails dangling toward her plate, and bit down on her bottom lip again. After a couple of beats, she looked up, eyes glistening with unshed tears. "I'm sorry for hurting your feelings."

Miranda's feelings were a mess, but that wasn't Emily's fault. "No, honey. You didn't hurt me. I'm just sad that you were afraid to talk to me about your father. I'd wondered why you didn't ask, and now I know. And no matter what anyone might say, you can always come to me with your questions."

"About my dad?"

"About anyone and anything." Miranda glanced

across the table at Uncle George. "Would you mind if I let you and Emily wash the dishes alone tonight?"

"Of course not." He blessed her with an affectionate smile, then turned to Emily and winked. "I know where your mama hid the chocolate chip cookies. And there's a brand new carton of vanilla ice cream in the freezer."

Miranda didn't usually let Emily eat sweets this close to bedtime, but she would gladly make an exception tonight. If the two dishwashers wolfed down a dozen cookies and a gallon of ice cream, she wouldn't complain.

After rinsing her plate in the sink, Miranda left the kitchen and headed down the hall until she reached Matt's bedroom. She held her breath, then knocked lightly on the door.

As footsteps, punctuated by the heart-wrenching tap of his cane, grew louder, her heart flipped and flopped in her chest like a trout on a hook, frantic to return to a safe, familiar environment. But she remained rooted to the floor, determined to face him, and waited for him to let her in.

When the door swung open, Matt stood before her, broad-shouldered, bare-chested and more muscular than she'd imagined. Her gaze drifted down his taut abs to his jeans, the top button undone. As much as she wanted to continue to take him in, to relish the manly changes that had taken place, she zeroed in on his eyes, once as clear and blue as the Texas sky, now a stormy winter gray.

He'd worn a similar expression the day her father

arrived at the Double G, raising hell and setting the breakup of their teenage romance in motion.

"I, uh…" She cleared her throat. "I need to talk to you. Can I come in?"

His only response was to step aside, cane in hand, and limp to his bed, where he took a seat on the edge of the mattress, leaving her to shut the door behind her.

Miranda scanned the room. The same rodeo posters and a schedule, long since outdated, still adorned the off-white walls. The maple chest of drawers and matching nightstand hadn't been moved. Even the familiar blue-plaid bedspread covered the double bed.

Too bad the angry cowboy glaring at her wasn't the same guy she used to know.

If only he were. She could have faced the *old* Matt in all honesty, without choosing her words, without holding back. She would have been able to fall into the comfort of his arms and tell him she was sorry for the delay in contacting him, for the hurt she'd unintentionally caused him—for the hurt she'd caused them both.

She leaned against the closed door. "I'm sorry. I should have told you about Emily sooner."

He rolled his eyes. "A *lot* sooner."

Right. "But I didn't tell her you'd died. Apparently, that was my father's doing."

Matt rolled his eyes. "I'm not surprised. Your dad never thought I was good enough for his little berry princess."

Talk about direct hits. She remained standing, clasped fists hanging at her side. "Just so you know, I didn't find out I was pregnant until after we broke up."

Matt crossed his arms and frowned. "You should have called me as soon as you knew."

"Yes, you're right. But if you remember, my dad limited my cell and telephone usage."

Matt chuffed at what sounded, even to her, like a lame excuse. "Your father didn't let you date, either. But you found a way around it."

True. She'd lied to her father, telling him time and again she was going to the library to meet with her study group. Her dishonesty hadn't sat well with her then—or now. But that was the only time she'd willfully deceived him. She had too much respect for him, for all he'd been through, all he'd accomplished in life. As a young boy, he'd gone to work with his father in the strawberry fields, learning the ins and outs of farming. When he grew up, he and his father purchased their own berry farm, then expanded it into an impressive operation with fields all over the state.

Matt slowly shook his head. "Your old man must have really blown a fuse when he found out you were going to have a baby, especially mine."

He certainly had. But going into detail about the early days of her pregnancy wasn't going to do anyone any good right now, so she cut to the chase. "He was smitten with Emily the very first minute he saw her and held her in his arms. And, for what it's worth, he's been a good grandfather to her."

Matt clicked his tongue. "Don't you think that lying to her about me ought to throw him out of the running for Grandfather of the Year?"

"If she'd asked me, I would have been honest. I

had no idea my father would tell her something like that. There was no reason for it. And it was way out of line."

"Sounds like you finally learned to stand up to him."

"I guess you could say that. But whenever I roll over, it's out of respect, not fear." She tucked a strand of hair behind her ear. "My dad was strict and expected a lot out of me, but he's a loving father and grandfather. I hope, one day, you'll be able to see that."

"Not gonna happen."

She supposed it wouldn't. Not for a long time, anyway.

"Does your old man know where you are?" Matt's harsh tone and narrowed gaze shot right to the heart of her. And so did his question.

She sucked in a deep breath, hoping the oxygen would clear her head and cleanse her soul, then slowly let it out. "Not exactly, but he knows we're safe. And that I'm staying with a friend."

Matt arched a brow.

"Okay," she admitted. "That could be considered a lie of omission. But believe it or not, I've always meant well and wanted the best for everyone involved."

So why had she begun to feel like the villainess in this mess?

While tempted to make her way to the edge of Matt's bed and sit beside him, she realized she'd have to earn the intimacy of his friendship. So she stood her ground and crossed her own arms. "I don't blame you for being angry at my dad—and not just because he told Emily you were dead. When we were kids, you saw a bad side of him."

"I don't care about your old man or the past. What's done is done."

"Okay, but I'd like to make things right."

Matt's gaze softened slightly, but not enough for her to make any assumptions or to move toward him.

"Is that why you came to the Double G?" he asked.

Not really. And not at first. But the compulsion to finally make things right was why she was standing in his room now. "Yes, that's pretty much why I'm here."

He nodded, then glanced at the cane that rested within reach on the edge of the mattress where he sat.

She placed her hand on her womb, caressing the small baby bump that she wouldn't be able to hide much longer with blousy tops and dresses. In fact, she'd suspected George already knew she was pregnant, since he was pretty observant. Not that he'd say anything.

When Matt looked up, she let her hand drop to her side and offered him a shy smile. "Like I said, I'm sorry. I should have told you that you were a father."

"You've got that right."

"I've made mistakes, but Emily isn't one of them. She's a great kid. So for now, let's focus on her."

"All right." Matt uncrossed his arms and raked a hand through his hair. "But just for the record, I would've done anything in my power to take care of you and Emily."

"I know." And that's why she'd walked away from him. Matt would have stood up to her father, challenged his threat, only to be knocked to his knees—and worse.

No, leaving town and cutting all ties with Matt was the only thing she could've done to protect him.

As she stood in the room where their daughter was conceived, as she studied the only man she'd ever loved, the memories crept up on her, the old feelings, too.

When she'd been sixteen, there'd been something about the fun-loving nineteen-year-old cowboy that had drawn her attention. And whatever it was continued to tug at her now. But she shook it off. Too many years had passed, too many tears had been shed.

Besides, an unwed, single mother who was expecting another man's baby wouldn't stand a chance with a champion bull rider who had his choice of pretty cowgirls. And she'd best not forget that.

"Aw, hell," Matt said, as he ran a hand through his hair again and blew out a weary sigh. "Maybe you did Emily a favor by leaving when you did. Who knows what kind of father I would have made back then. Or even now."

At that, Miranda longed to cross the room and take his hands in hers. The Matt she used to know would have been a great dad. And something told her the new Matt would be, too.

But he was a rodeo star now, with all the good and bad that came with it. So if he wanted to be a part of Emily's life, what kind of role model would he be?

But that was beside the point. He deserved a chance to know his daughter.

"Matt," she said, "I think you're going to be an awesome father, if you want to be. Either way, I'm going to talk to Emily and tell her that her *abuelito* was mistaken, that her father is very much alive."

"So you're going to tell her that I'm her father?"

"Yes." She eyed him carefully. "Unless you'd rather I didn't."

He didn't respond right away. Was the decision that hard for him to make?

When he glanced up, his gaze seemed to zero in on hers. But this time, it wasn't in anger. "I'd like to be there when you tell her. If that's okay."

She blew out a breath she hadn't realized she'd been holding. "Of course. I think that would be best."

For the first time since Matt arrived home, his expression grew familiar. Not completely, but enough to remind her of the old Matt and to stir up old feelings. But she'd better keep her wits about her—and her emotions in check.

"When should we tell her?" he asked.

"Whenever you're ready."

He nodded pensively. "Tomorrow, I guess."

"Okay then." She managed a smile. "I'll see you at breakfast."

Then she turned and let herself out of his room. The hard part was over.

Or was it?

It was one thing to think they'd be able to co-parent their daughter. But what about a child that wasn't his? The future and the possible so-called family dynamics were worrisome at best.

And what about those sexy buckle bunnies who thought Max was God's gift to womanhood?

No way could Miranda ever compete with them, especially as her pregnancy advanced, as new stretch marks developed...

She swore under her breath. Now that she'd opened up a Pandora's box of emotion—real or imagined—she had no idea how much her heart or her ego could bear.

Chapter Three

Last night, after talking to Matt, Miranda had turned in early, emotionally exhausted. But she'd barely slept a wink. Memories—both the good and the bad, happy and sad—plagued her, making it impossible for her to unwind.

When she finally dozed off, her dreams refused to let her rest.

Sirens and flashing lights.

The snap of handcuffs.

A gavel banging down. Again and again.

A cell door clanging shut.

Knees hitting the courtroom floor. A sobbing voice screaming, No!

Miranda shot up, her heart racing, her brow damp from perspiration. She'd had that nightmare before, but it hadn't been so real.

Once her pulse slowed to normal and her eyes adjusted to the predawn darkness, she threw off the covers, got out of bed and padded to the bathroom, where she washed her face, brushed her hair and dressed for the day. She chose the maternity jeans and a blousy pink T-shirt she'd purchased in town last week, after her last obstetrical appointment.

Most pregnant women liked showing off their baby bumps, but Miranda wasn't one of them. Not now. Not yet.

It wasn't that she didn't want the baby—a little boy she planned to name after her father, which might soften the blow when she told him she was expecting. It's just that she hadn't wanted the news to leak out. If Gavin learned that she was having his son, he might want shared custody.

As she headed for the kitchen, she relished the aroma of fresh-brewed coffee and ham sizzling in a pan.

George stood in front of the stove, while Emily—her hair pulled into an off-centered ponytail and adorned with a red ribbon—sat on the counter next to him and chattered away about what she and Sweetie Pie planned to do today.

"Good morning," Miranda said. "You two are awake earlier than usual."

"Emily usually gets up first," George said, "but I figured I'd better get busy this morning and fix a hearty breakfast. Matt's looking a little puny."

He'd looked pretty darn healthy last night when he'd answered the bedroom door bare-chested.

George adjusted the flame under the blackened,

cast-iron skillet, then turned to Miranda with a smile. "I found my mother's old recipe box last night. I won't have much use for it, but I thought you might like to… look it over. She was one heck of a cook."

"I'd love to see her recipes. And if there's a special meal or dish you'd like me to make, I'd be happy to give it a try."

George laughed. "I'd hoped you'd say that." Then he nodded toward the teapot. "The whistle isn't blowing yet, but the water should be ready. How 'bout I pour you a cup?"

"Thanks. That would be nice." Miranda made her way to the pantry and retrieved a box of herbal tea bags. She'd no more than turned around when Matt entered the kitchen, fresh from the shower and looking more handsome than ever.

He gave her a distracted nod, then using his cane, limped to the coffee maker and filled a cup to the brim.

Miranda placed a hand on her baby bump, which seemed to have doubled in size overnight. She supposed that was to be expected, now that she was approaching her fifth month. She hadn't given the maternal habit much thought before, but she'd better be careful not to draw any undue attention to her condition. So she quickly removed her hand and stole a glance at Matt, who was watching her over the rim of his coffee mug, his brow furrowed.

Her cheeks warmed, and her heart thumped. Did he suspect…?

Not that it mattered. He'd find out soon enough.

She took the cup of hot water George had poured

for her and carried it to the scarred antique table and took a seat.

While her tea steeped, neither she nor Matt said a word. But she imagined him saying, *Apparently, you have a habit of running away from your baby daddies.*

Just the thought of him having a reaction like that struck a hard blow, a low one. But then again, she couldn't blame him for being angry, resentful. Judgmental.

And he didn't even have to say anything to her. As it was, she felt guilty enough, which was why she wasn't looking forward to facing her father and announcing she was, once again, unmarried and pregnant.

Nor was she ready to admit to Matt that she was having another man's baby.

As Matt took his first sip of coffee, he studied Miranda, who looked a little pale, if not green around the gills. But so what? She deserved to feel guilty. She'd kept his daughter away from him for years.

Carlos Contreras, the Texas berry king, had made it perfectly clear that, at least in his opinion, Matt wasn't good enough for his precious daughter. And apparently, Princess Miranda felt the same way.

Miranda's deceit and the unfairness of it all rose up like an index finger and poked at his chest, jabbing at an old wound that, apparently, hadn't healed. It hurt like hell to know he'd been shut out of a family once again.

Last night, after Miranda came to his bedroom and admitted that Emily was his, a secret she'd kept for nine years, Matt hadn't been able to sleep a wink. He'd even

popped a couple of the pain pills the doctor had pre-
scribed and he rarely used. But even that hadn't helped.
Not when the real pain had very little to do with his knee.

He kept rehashing old conversations he'd put to rest
years ago, like the last one he and Miranda had had.

Let's take a break for a little while, Miranda had
said. *I'll call you when Daddy's cooled down and had
a chance to think things over.*

But that call never came.

Matt leaned his left hip against the cupboard under
the kitchen counter, taking the weight off his left knee.
He lifted his mug, but didn't take a drink. Instead, he
gazed at Miranda. She'd grown prettier with each passing year. Even in a pair of loose-fitting blue jeans and
a baggy T-shirt, she was a knockout.

Her waist, once flat and perfect, had a paunch now.
He'd noticed it before and had assumed it was to be expected after having a baby. That is, until she'd caught
him watching her a few moments ago. An uneasy expression crossed her face, and the hand that had been
resting on her rounded stomach dropped to her side.

Was she pregnant?

She might be, but he'd never ask.

All he knew was what Uncle George had told him
yesterday. She'd recently ended a relationship and
needed time to think.

She sure looked pensive this morning, as she stirred
a teaspoon in her cup long after any sugar had dis-
solved.

What was she thinking about? Whether she should
reconcile with her ex?

Or had she deserted another expectant father, leaving him completely unaware of her pregnancy? That is, if Matt's suspicion was right.

He glanced at his uncle, who was cracking eggs into the skillet he'd used to fry ham. Did he know more about Miranda's condition, her situation, than he'd let on?

He had to, since he'd clearly taken her under his wing, going so far as to provide housing and food for her and Emily, not to mention hosting a menagerie.

Then again, his uncle had always liked Miranda. *That lil' gal has a sweet way about her, Matt. She's smart and funny, too. If I'd had a daughter, I'd want her to be just like her.*

And Miranda had felt the same way about Uncle George, too. Or so she'd said.

Matt turned his focus to Emily, who kept glancing out the kitchen window, then at the clock on the microwave.

She was a cute kid. He couldn't say that she looked like him, other than maybe the shape of her eyes—but not the color. Still, he didn't doubt that he was her father. The only doubt he actually had was whether he could be the kind of dad she deserved.

The dog padded through the kitchen and into the service porch. It whined a couple of times and scratched at the back door. Since no one else seemed to notice, Matt reached for his cane and headed to the service porch to let it out.

"No!" Emily jumped down from her perch on the counter, where she'd been watching George fry eggs, and ran to the door, grabbing the dog by the collar before it could go outside to pee.

What the hell?

"Sweetie Pie can't go outside until the sun comes up," Emily said, her voice coming out in short frantic huffs. "Or else she'll chase that skunk again. And she always gets sprayed and stinky."

"Always?" Matt asked. "How many times has she gotten sprayed?"

"Four." Emily knelt before the dog, cupped her furry face and made kissy sounds. "Wait a little bit longer, Sweetie Pie. I'll open the door as soon as it gets light and after that ornery ol' skunk goes to sleep."

A grin tugged at Matt's lip, and he slowly shook his head. "You'd think that getting a snout full of *Eau de Stink* more than twice would have convinced her to try chasing another critter."

Emily looked up at him, her sweet smile reaching into his chest and touching something soft and tender.

"You got that right," George called out from the kitchen. "Good ol' Lulu Belle was a smart dog, but Sweetie Pie is a slow learner."

Back in the day, Matt had been one, too. You'd think that, after his widowed dad had remarried and chosen his stepbrother over him, Matt would have known better than to harbor thoughts of family, hearth and home. But then he'd met Miranda, and she'd stomped on his wounded heart, leaving him feeling abandoned yet again.

Fortunately, Matt didn't need to get sprayed a third time before learning his lesson.

While refilling his cup, he studied his daughter. What would she say when she learned that Matt was her father?

And when would they tell her?

He stole a glance at Miranda, who hadn't said much of anything, even when she wasn't sipping from her fancy china teacup that used to belong to George's mother. He had no idea what she planned to do with her life. Her decisions were none of his business.

That is, unless they affected Emily. And if he didn't agree with the choices Miranda made—*or any her father made*, Matt wasn't about to sit on the sidelines and let them dictate his daughter's life. And if they thought they could shut him out, like they'd done so far, there'd be hell to pay.

By the time breakfast was on the table, the sun had risen and Sweetie Pie had gone outside to take care of her doggy business and to go in search of her black-and-white-striped nemesis.

None of the adults spoke while they ate their fill of ham and scrambled eggs, but Emily chattered away. And Matt hung on her every word.

As she chomped on a piece of ham, her eyes brightened. "Guess what? You know Suzy Reinquist, the new girl who brought an arrowhead to school for show-and-tell? She has six toes on each foot."

"Emily," Matilda said, "please don't talk with your mouth full."

The child swallowed, chased it down with a sip of orange juice and continued her story. "I didn't believe

Suzy when she told us, 'cause that would make twelve toes, and everyone knows you only have ten. But then she took off her shoes and socks so we could count them. And sure enough…"

Even if Emily weren't his daughter, Matt would have enjoyed listening to her. She had a unique way of seeing the world. And he liked hearing about her interests and friends.

Emily took another swig of juice. "I can't wait for spring break to get over. I love school. I like Mrs. Crowley, too. But she wasn't at school on Friday. We had a substitute. I forget her name, but she's kind of old and has a little bald spot on the back of her head. I didn't notice it until she turned around to write our math assignment on the board."

Before the girl could share another story, Uncle George pushed his chair away from the table. "You'll have to excuse me. The ranch hands will be arriving soon, and I need to get to work."

"Me, too." Emily downed the rest of her OJ, then got to her feet. "The chickens laid three eggs yesterday. I wonder how many I'll find today."

"Honey, wait a minute." Miranda glanced at Matt, then back at their daughter. "I have something I need to talk to you about."

"Am I in trouble again?" Emily placed her hands on her hips and frowned.

"No, you're not in trouble," Miranda said.

"Then can we wait until I check on Dumpling? The other chickens kept pecking at her yesterday."

Miranda rested her forearms on the table and leaned

forward. "No, honey. I've already waited too long to tell you."

Emily plopped back into her seat. "What is it?"

Miranda glanced at Matt, then focused on their daughter. "Your *abuelito* was wrong when he told you that your father died."

Emily cocked her head and furrowed her brow. "You mean my father *isn't* dead?"

"No. In fact, he didn't even know about you until recently."

Emily crossed her arms, leaned back in her seat and frowned. "Does *Abuelito* know that?"

Miranda nodded.

Emily's eyes widened. "You mean he *lied* to me?"

"Yes." Miranda drew in a deep breath, then slowly let it out. "I'm afraid he did."

Emily remained silent for a beat, then she rolled her eyes. "That *really* makes me mad. He told me to always tell the truth, no matter how hard it is. But then *he* didn't."

"I'm sorry," Miranda said. "That was wrong of him."

To say the least. Matt continued to watch the conversation unfold, his interest in his daughter growing. The kid had spunk. He liked that.

"I'm going to let your grandfather know how I feel, how we both feel about him lying to you the next time I see him."

That didn't seem to appease the child. But hell, why should it?

"Just so you know," Miranda added, "I'd planned

to tell you about your father when you asked me about him. But I shouldn't have waited."

"So where *is* my dad? And how come he didn't know about me? If he did, maybe he would have come to see me or called or…something." Emily shook her head, her ponytail swishing from side to side. "Does he even know when my birthday is?"

"It's August the third," Matt said. "And I'm going to try my best to be with you on that day from now on."

Emily's lips parted, and when she turned to him, her eyes widened in disbelief. "*You?* You're my dad?"

Damn. Did the kid not approve of him, either? Grave Digger had done a real number on Matt's body when he stomped on him, casting a shadow on all he'd accomplished, all the buckles he'd won. But Miranda's rejection, her father's disapproval and now Emily's reaction crushed him in a way that blasted bull hadn't.

"Yes," Matt said. "I'm your dad."

Emily eyed him carefully, taking in the news that had thrown him for a loop when he'd first heard it last night.

He held his breath as he awaited her response. For some reason, her assessment of him concerned him more than that of any high school principal, police officer or courtroom judge.

The crease in the girl's brow deepened, then she looked down at her empty plate, studying the smears of ham drippings as if they were tea leaves.

When she finally looked up, her expression eased into one of cautious curiosity. "Why didn't you know about me? Didn't you ever want a little girl?"

He could throw her mother and grandfather under the

bus, but that might make things even worse. "I'm here now. And I'm glad I finally got to meet my daughter."

She seemed to chew on that for a beat, then asked, "Does that mean you're coming to my birthday party?"

"You bet I will. I'll even bring a present. What would you like?"

She shrugged. "I don't need anything."

"Not even a bicycle?"

At that, she smiled. "I have a pony, remember?"

"Right. And you're going to be a cowgirl when you grow up."

"Yep. But I might be a veterinarian. That's a doctor for animals." She glanced at her mother. "Can I go now?"

That was it? She'd moved on to gathering eggs rather than locking in a birthday present? Hell, he was tempted to bring her nine of them, one for each birthday he'd missed.

When Miranda nodded, Emily turned to Matt and smiled. "You wanna go with me to get the eggs?"

A farm chore had never sounded so appealing. "I'd like that." In fact, he liked it a lot.

She got up from her chair, then walked out to the service porch. Matt glanced at Miranda, assuming she'd want to join them, but she shook her head and waved him off, allowing him some privacy when meeting his daughter for the first time.

He appreciated that, even though his anger and resentment hadn't diminished too much. Maybe, in time, he'd find it easier to forgive her than he'd thought.

As he followed Emily outside, she turned and

blessed him with a dimpled smile. "Want me to show you my pony and my lamb before we get the eggs?"

"Absolutely."

As they walked toward the corral, she pointed to his cane. "Why are you limping?"

"I tried to ride an ornery bull, but he didn't like it. So he threw me off and stepped on me."

She stopped in her tracks and turned to face him. "That wasn't very smart. You do know that bulls are dangerous, right?"

"Yeah. I know."

"You're lucky he didn't poke you with his horns and stomp you to death. And then I wouldn't have got to meet you at all." She lifted her index finger and wagged it at him, a gesture that touched his heart. "So don't do it again, okay? I just found you and don't want you to get hurt or die."

He couldn't help chuckling at her admonition. As much as he'd have liked to respect her wishes, he couldn't give up the rodeo. If he wasn't a champion bull rider, who was he? But she'd given him something to think about.

When they reached the corral, where the black-and-white Shetland pony munched on alfalfa that George must have fed him this morning, Emily pointed to the little gelding. "That's Oreo. Do you know why we call him that?"

"Let me guess." A grin stretched across Matt's face. "Because he eats cookies?"

She laughed. "No, silly. Because he looks like one. An Oreo cookie. Get it?"

"Aw. Yes. That's very clever. Did you name him?"

"No, the people who owned him before Uncle George bought him for me called him that. But I got to name Bob and the chickens."

"Is Bob the lamb?"

"Yep."

"Maybe you should have called him Baaaab?"

"You're funny!" Her smile darn near turned him inside out.

He'd always liked to make his friends laugh—and he did so often. But the pleasure he'd taken at seeing their happy adult faces paled in comparison to hearing the lilt of Emily's sweet laugh and seeing the bright-eyed smile that dimpled her cheeks.

"Come on," she said. "I want you to meet him. And you can watch me feed him."

"Uncle George doesn't do that for you?"

"Oh, no! I take care of Bob all by myself. I feed him and give him water and bathe him and everything. I'm going to show him at the fair. He's very cool, and he likes going for walks. He's my best friend. But don't tell Sweetie Pie."

A grin tugged at Matt's lips, although he tried to hide it. Implying that Emily might not be pulling her weight when it came to the ranch chores seemed to have horrified her, which filled him with a bit of pride. He would have felt the same way, when he'd first moved onto the Double G as a young teen.

After feeding Bob, Emily reached into her back pocket, whipped out a pink Western bandana and tied it to the lamb's neck. Then she led Matt to the chicken coop and pointed out each one. "That's Dumpling. And the brown and black one is Nuggets. Pot Pie is behind the coop and the one drinking water is Casserole."

"They're all named after chicken dishes, huh? Does that mean you're going to eat them?"

"No!" Her once happy expression morphed into one that was just as horrified as the last. "They're my friends. Besides, they give us eggs."

The little girl—*his* little girl—was a hoot. Smart as a whip, spunky and pretty to boot. And in spite of feeling awkward around her earlier, she'd managed to put him at ease.

Not that he expected to take to fatherhood the way he'd taken to riding a horse or roping cattle, but taking on a paternal role didn't seem nearly as scary as it had when he first learned he had a child.

Emily unlatched the door to the coop and went inside to check for eggs, but came back empty-handed.

"Looks like the girls aren't doing their jobs."

Emily shrugged. "Sometimes they don't lay them until later. That's why I check for eggs all the time."

After shutting the wired door and hooking the latch, she brushed her hands on her denim-clad thighs. When she looked up, her eyes sparkled. "You know what? I'm really going to like having a daddy."

Something deep in his heart warmed at the comment, the acceptance.

"I'm glad to hear that," he said. "I'm going to like having a daughter." Surprisingly, those words rang true.

He couldn't ask for more in a child, other than wishing he'd known about her when she'd been a baby. But there wasn't anything he could do about that now.

They did have today, and each one after this. Yet while he could envision himself bonding with Emily, he wasn't so sure how he felt about her mother.

Emily stopped and gazed up at him. "You don't believe in hitting kids, do you?"

He hadn't seen that question coming. "No, I don't."

"Good. That's why I don't like Gavin."

Matt's gut twisted into a knot, his senses on high alert, and he braced himself for her answer. "Who's Gavin?"

"The guy my mom was going to marry. I'm glad she didn't. Gavin wouldn't be a good daddy."

Matt stiffened. "Why do you say that?"

"Because he's a yeller. And a hitter."

The knot in his gut was nothing compared to the clench of his fists. "Did he hit you or your mom?"

"Only me. And he made my nose bleed."

A chill ran through Matt's veins. How dare that man hit a child. Especially *this* child.

"I really wanted to be a flower girl," Emily added. "And I really liked the dress I was going to wear. But not if we married Gavin."

"Is that why your mom left him?"

Emily nodded. "Yep. Because he hit me for crying when I had an earache."

Matt's gut clenched. What kind of monster had Miranda planned to marry?

"*Abuelito*, my grandfather, was mad, too," Emily added.

"At Gavin?"

"No. At my mom. Because he had to pay a whole lot of money for the wedding, even though no one went to it."

That figured. A snide comment formed on the tip of Matt's tongue, but he clamped his mouth shut until the urge to blurt it out passed.

"So where did your mom meet Gavin?" he asked.

"At *Abuelito's* Christmas party."

Matt glanced over his shoulder at the house, wondering if Miranda had come out to the porch to see how he and Emily were doing. He supposed he should be grateful that she'd allowed them to have this precious time alone. But he no longer wanted time with his daughter. He now wanted to get the straight scoop from Miranda.

No doubt she had made the right decision to leave. Had she pressed charges? She certainly should have. Questions began to pop up in his mind, one after another.

Why had it taken her so long to see through Gavin?

And how had she gotten involved with a guy like that in the first place?

As soon as Emily was out of earshot, Matt intended to learn the answer to all his questions. And in this case, he wouldn't be the least bit reluctant to pry.

Chapter Four

Miranda wanted nothing more than to go outside with Matt and Emily, to listen to their conversation and to watch their facial expressions, but she'd been reluctant to ask if she could join them. She'd kept Emily to herself for so long that it only seemed fair to let Matt have some time with their daughter without her hovering nearby.

But that didn't mean she'd go so far as to hole up in the home office, balancing the checkbook and paying the monthly bills. Instead, she brought her work to the kitchen and sat close to the back door, where she expected them to reenter the house after Emily showed Matt around the ranch and introduced him to her barnyard *friends*.

And while she had plenty to keep her busy, she

found it difficult to focus on anything other than the tour going on outside, on the possible conversations unfolding between Emily and her father.

Finally, the back door creaked open, and her heart dropped with a thud. For a moment, she froze like a possum in the headlights of an oncoming big rig.

As approaching footsteps sounded, her pulse throbbed harder and more intense with each tap of a cane. She turned away from the laptop screen, as if she'd been completely taken aback by Matt's and her daughter's entrance, and her eyes widened as if to say, *Oh. It's you.*

"We're back!" Emily's dimpled grin, the bounce in her step and the swish of her ponytail suggested the tour had gone well. On the other hand, Matt's expression was a little too solemn for a man who'd enjoyed his time outdoors with their daughter.

"Mom," Emily said, "can I ride Oreo? I wanna show my dad how I can saddle and bridle her all by myself."

Miranda arched a brow at Matt. "Are you okay with that?"

"Sure." He made his way toward the kitchen table, his very presence sucking the air from the room.

He might have just agreed to go back out to the corral with Emily, but Miranda wasn't convinced that he was actually *okay* with it. But then again, maybe his knee was bothering him. And if so, he'd probably appreciate having some time to sit down for a while and take the weight off his bad leg.

"All right," Miranda told their eager daughter. "You can ride your pony, but not until you clean your room."

"Aw, man." Emily let out a dramatic pout that lasted all of two beats, then she turned to Matt. "Will you wait? It won't take me very long."

"I'll be here."

As the child dashed off, Matt took a seat across from her and leaned his cane against the wall.

"How did it go?" she asked.

"It went great." He stretched out his bad leg, leaned back in his chair and zeroed in on her with a piercing gaze. "That is, until Emily told me that guy you were going to marry hit her and bloodied her nose."

Wow. Nothing like cutting right to the chase. But Miranda couldn't blame him. She'd been furious, shaken to the core, when she'd learned what Gavin had done. Not only had she been angry with him, she'd blamed herself for not seeing the signs sooner.

"I was appalled, too," she said. "That's why I left him."

Silence stretched between them, slowly sucking the air from the room, until Matt said, "Dammit, Miranda. What'd you ever see in a guy who'd do something like that?"

"I've asked myself that a hundred times. But he was sweet at first. We met at the company Christmas party a year before last."

"So he was a charmer, huh? Swept you off your feet?"

"In a way." In truth, the only one who'd ever swept her off her feet had been Matt, when he'd been in his senior year and she'd transferred to his high school as a sophomore. The first time she'd spotted him, looked into those bright blue eyes and saw that sweet but cocky grin, she'd been moonstruck.

But there was no point in reminding him how they'd once felt about each other. Matt had clearly moved on, and so had she.

"It might surprise you," she said, "to know that Gavin was wearing a Santa Claus suit that night and passing out candy canes."

Matt rolled his eyes. "Ho, ho, ho."

She understood his anger, his frustration, his concern, but before she could respond, Emily returned to the kitchen, wearing a bright-eyed smile, as well as the new boots and child-size black cowboy hat George had surprised her with last week. But Miranda knew her daughter's tricks when it came to having a higher priority than a tidy room.

"You know," Miranda said, "I'm going to look in the closet and under the bed. So you might want to double check and make sure you did a good job picking up."

Emily folded her arms across her chest and shifted her weight to one foot. "Can't I do that *after* I ride Oreo?"

"I'm afraid not. And when you're finished, please bring your hamper to the service porch so I can wash your clothes."

Emily let out an exasperated sigh, then turned to Matt. "I'll be back. It'll just be a few more minutes."

"I'm not going anywhere," he said.

After Emily skipped out of the kitchen, Matt zeroed in on Miranda again, the intensity of his gaze threatening to undo her. "I hate bullies. Always have, always will. And if that guy was standing here right now, I'd be tempted to take a couple of swings at him for hitting a child."

She'd watched him stand up for the underdog on quite a few occasions, one of which had landed him in detention. He'd been a real hero back then. Still was, she suspected.

Matt slowly shook his head. "I don't understand, Miranda. There had to have been signs that he had a mean streak."

"Not at first. But I have to admit a few red flags popped up during the last six weeks we were together."

"Like what?"

She felt compelled to tell him it wasn't any of his business, but then again, she wanted to assure him that she'd never willingly put her child in jeopardy. "Gavin began drinking more in the evenings and blamed it on stress at work. He'd always liked his scotch, but it became a nightly habit. And whenever he'd had too much, which seemed to be most nights, he'd snap at whoever he was talking to—a client on the telephone, me… Emily. It was then that I realized he had a temper, although I'd never realized he'd become physically violent."

For the first time since Matt arrived on the Double G, his expression softened, and he began to remind her of the old Matt, the one who'd been her best friend.

"Then why didn't you break up with him six weeks sooner?"

The *real* reason? She hated to admit it, but she hadn't wanted to disappoint Gavin's mother or her father. They'd both been over the moon about the marriage. Her dad considered it a business merger of sorts He'd tried for years to convince Gavin's father to invest in a farming venture in Mexico, and their partnership was finally coming together. Then there was Gavin's mom, who considered her only child's wedding to be a huge social event, one she'd been dreaming of since the day he was born. And since the woman was recovering from a recent mastectomy, Miranda hadn't wanted to disappoint her or create any additional stress on her health. But none of that mattered the day she learned Gavin had not only hit Emily, but that it hadn't been the first time.

"I wish I had canceled the wedding sooner," she said. "And for more reasons than one."

Matt remained silent, his eyes holding judgment.

Miranda took in a deep, fortifying breath, then slowly let it out. "There were only about seventy-five people on the original invitation list, which was about all my dad's backyard could hold. But before I could blink, that number quadrupled, and we needed a bigger venue. So my dad put down a huge non-refundable deposit so we could hold it at a country club." And not just any club, but the nicest and most exclusive in San Antonio.

Matt leaned forward and rested his forearms—stronger, bulkier than she remembered—on the table. "Sounds like things got way out of hand."

"To say the least." Gavin's mother had gotten so involved in planning the ceremony and reception that she'd hardly talked or thought about anything else. On the upside, it had taken her mind off her health issues and pulled her out of the resulting depression that followed her surgery.

Miranda didn't dare mention the flowers they'd ordered from Europe or the designer gown that had been altered. And who knew what they'd done with the white doves Gavin's mother had insisted would be a nice touch.

"I'll admit that I should have put my foot down a lot sooner," Miranda said, "but the closer it got to Valentine's Day, the worse I felt about calling it off."

"I'm glad you finally did."

Was he? She tried to read into his words, his expression, then she shook it off. Her curiosity was sure to lead her down a path she had no business taking. Not after all this time.

She glanced down at the table, where her clasped hands rested, then she risked a glance at Matt. His gaze locked on hers, and she spotted something other than anger in his eyes. Sympathy? Concern?

For a moment, he was the old Matt who'd swept her off her feet in high school. And while they'd never be lovers again, maybe, just maybe they could be friends.

"Did Gavin ever hit *you*?" he asked, as if nothing had changed, as if he still had her back. "Did he threaten you in any way?"

"No. He raised his voice a couple of times. But he never got physical with me."

"But given time," Matt said, "he probably would have. And he definitely would have hurt Emily again. Did you press charges against him?"

"I seriously thought about it, but my dad talked me out of it."

The crease in Matt's brow deepened, and any sign of sympathy faded from his eyes. "Are you *kidding*? Why in the hell would he talk you out of it? And worse, why would you let him?"

"When I told my dad why I'd broken our engagement, he completely understood. And he was angry at Gavin, too. But Gavin's father is one of the investors in a joint farming venture, a big one, and my dad didn't want to complicate matters. I would have argued with him, but I'd already broken our engagement, and since I'd left town, I knew Emily was safe."

Matt flinched, and his eye twitched. She wasn't sure what he was thinking—or feeling—but she reached out and placed her hand on his forearm, a bold move she hadn't planned, one she wasn't sure how to take back.

"Don't worry, Matt. When I left Gavin, it was for good. And if he ever came around and tried to talk to me, I wouldn't hesitate to file a restraining order or press charges."

Concern swept across Matt's brow once more, and she was tempted to stroke his arm rather than hold her hand in place. But she didn't.

"Do you *expect* him to come after you?" he asked.

"Maybe." She wouldn't put it past him. He'd called several times after she left, and when his apologies and pleas became demands, she blocked his number. "But he'd have to find me first. And no one knows I'm here."

The muscles in his forearm flexed, and she removed her hand, breaking the physical connection she had no right to make. She fingered the scarred surface of the antique kitchen table instead.

"No one?" His head tilted slightly.

She slowly shook her head. "Not even my dad. All I told him was that I needed to spend some time away from San Antonio and the office, but I didn't tell him where I was staying."

Matt rolled his eyes and let out a humph. "He'd burst an artery if he knew you were here."

"Probably. At first. But he'd get over it." Eventually, anyway.

"So what are you waiting for?"

"I don't want to tell him until I have a solid plan for the future." A future that now included Gavin's baby, something else her father didn't know. Yet. "But my plans are coming together."

"So what's your next move?"

"Finding a job and a place to live. I can't stay on the Double G forever, and I don't want to go back to my condo in San Antonio." Only trouble was, she couldn't put any of that into motion until after the baby was born.

She'd also have to level with her father and tell him where she was staying. She'd then have to tell him she was pregnant and that he was going to be a grandfather again, which would both set him off and please him. But she'd had enough confessions for one day. She'd call him tomorrow.

"So…" She took another deep breath and slowly let it out. "How did things go when you went outside with Emily? How are you feeling about…?"

"Instant fatherhood?" He shrugged. "That's left to be seen. But Emily is a great kid. You've done a good job with her."

"Thanks."

His gaze locked on hers, stirring old memories, old feelings. "I wish I'd known her sooner."

"Believe it or not, so do I."

He studied her for a couple of beats, as if judging her sincerity. But she meant those words from the bottom of her heart. If she could go back in time and make other decisions, handle things differently than she had, she would. But other than telling Matt about Emily sooner, she would still make the same choices she'd made before. And for the same reasons.

"All done!" Emily called out, as she skipped into the kitchen.

Miranda's hand slipped from the tabletop to her baby bump. She usually found comfort in caressing her little one, but it didn't seem to help today. Instead, it only served to remind her that life went on.

And that there were no do-overs.

When Matt first entered the kitchen after his tour of Emily's barnyard menagerie, he'd been angry and resentful, along with a few other emotions he couldn't put his finger on, all of them equally negative. But after confronting Miranda, after gazing into her pretty brown eyes and feeling her gentle touch, he'd begun to sympathize. In fact, he'd begun to soften so much toward her that he was thankful for an interruption, even if it was the pitter-patter of little cowboy boots.

Matt turned away from Miranda, breaking whatever fragile tie they'd just had, and focused on their daughter. With her olive complexion, dark brown hair and hazel eyes, Emily looked a lot like her mother.

Lucky kid. Miranda had been a beautiful teenager, and she was even more so now. The years had been damn good to her. Or maybe he'd just forgotten how attractive she was.

Emily took after him, too, he supposed—the shape of her nose, the dimples in her cheeks. Not to mention the occasional mischievous spark that lit her eyes.

"I've got my room all cleaned up now," Emily said, as she entered the kitchen carrying a laundry basket. "Even the closet. And there's nothing under the bed anymore. So now can me and Matt—I mean, my dad— go outside?"

"Yes, you can. But please take that basket to the service porch and leave it next to the washer." Miranda blessed the girl with a dazzling smile, a heart-strumming display Matt hadn't seen in a long time, one he'd never expected to see again. A smile that threatened to turn him inside out like it once had.

He reached for his cane and got to his feet. "All right then. Looks like it's time to cowgirl up."

"Yes! *Finally*. Let's go." Emily led the way to the service porch, where she deposited the laundry basket. On the way out the back door, she glanced over her shoulder and smiled. "I like the way you rodeo talk, because I want to be a barrel racer when I get a little older and my mom lets me get a bigger horse."

"If it's okay with your mom, I'd be happy to work

with you while I'm here." Matt stole one last glance at Miranda, who nodded her approval.

Apparently, she had faith in him, which was a relief. But it wasn't his horsemanship that worried him. He could do that in his sleep. On the other hand, he hadn't planned to be a father. And a relationship like that was going to take a bit more work.

His gaze dropped to Miranda's lap, where one hand rested and the other caressed her rounded stomach. At first, he'd noticed what he'd thought was a paunch, the lingering evidence of childbirth. But then he'd realized the bulge didn't appear to be soft or flabby.

He'd wondered if she was pregnant, but there wasn't any doubt about it now. That was definitely a baby bump.

Did Gavin know? Was that the real reason she was hiding out at the Double G? Was she afraid for the baby?

If so, she'd be safe here. Especially while Matt was around. Bum knee or not, that bully wouldn't stand a chance.

Then again, Uncle George had never had a problem pulling his shotgun off the rack over the fireplace and chasing off an uninvited guest. He'd give that jerk a run for his money, too.

"Are you coming?" Emily called out from the open back door. "I'm letting in flies, and Uncle George is going to get mad. And he's already in a bad mood because he can't find the keys to his truck."

"I'd never want to set off Uncle George." Matt followed his daughter outside.

Okay, cowboy. Now it's time to Daddy up.

* * *

Miranda watched Matt and Emily leave the house until they shut the back door behind them. Should she join them this time? If Emily was going to ride Oreo, Matt's attention would be focused on her. So it's not like Miranda would be intruding on their conversation.

She'd give them a few minutes alone, then go out and check on them. She'd no more than made that decision when Uncle George entered the kitchen, grumbling as he passed her and made his way to the service porch, where he searched the key rack near the door, only to come up empty-handed.

"Looking for something?" she asked.

"I can't find the blasted keys to my truck. I could have sworn I left them hanging right here. Dammit." He slapped his gnarly hands on his hips and then brightened. "Oh, for Pete's sake." He reached into his pocket. "Here they are."

Miranda bit back a chuckle. "Where are you going?"

"I've gotta run a couple of errands in town."

"If you're going anywhere near the post office, we're going to need another roll of stamps. I'd like to mail out the monthly bills tomorrow."

"You got it."

"Will you be home for lunch?" she asked. Not that she planned on making anything other than sandwiches.

"Yeah, I'll be back. But don't bother fixing anything to eat. I'll pick up a couple pizzas. Better yet, I'll get something from that new restaurant near the Night Owl

Motel. I ordered the hot wings last time I was there, and that was the best cluckin' chicken I ever ate."

This time, Miranda let the laughter flow. Uncle George wasn't just a hoot, he was special. One of a kind. How could a man be sweet and gruff, soft and tough, all at the same time?

"If you don't mind," she said, "I think I'll watch Emily ride Oreo for a while, then I'll finish the office work."

"Suit yourself. You're the one balancing the books. I'm just glad I don't have to do it anymore—or worry that someone is robbing me blind."

"And I'm glad you let me and Emily stay here for the time being."

George grimaced, then stroked his left arm from shoulder to elbow and back again.

"What's the matter?" she asked. "Is your arm bothering you?"

"I slept on it wrong. It's nothin' that a couple of ibuprofen won't take care of." He nodded toward the door. "It's burnin' daylight. I gotta go."

"If you give me a minute," she said, "I can drive you."

"Oh, hell's bells. I might be old, but I'm not an invalid. And if you don't stop fussin' over me, the only place you're going to drive me is crazy." He punctuated his snarky tone with a wink, then he opened the back door and let himself out.

After stopping in the service porch, reaching into Emily's laundry basket and placing a load of colors into the washer, Miranda went outside, too, where she found Matt leaning against the corral, his cane propped up next to him, as he watched Emily saddle her pony.

She took a minute to study the cowboy from a distance, the way his hat tilted just right. The way he cocked his head. The way the sun lit the blond streaks in his light brown hair. Broad shoulders, narrow hips. If he'd just turn a bit to the right, she'd catch sight of his profile, of his handsome face...

That's enough of that, she told herself as she shook off her star-crossed attraction and headed toward him. When she reached his side, she lifted her hand to her forehead to shield the morning sun from her eyes.

"How's she doing?" she asked.

"She's a chip off the old block."

Miranda's heart swelled. She'd noticed so many of Matt's mannerisms in Emily, and she was glad he'd spotted them, too. "You're right. She really does take after you."

Matt turned toward her, providing that glimpse of his gorgeous face, and tossed her a playful grin. "The *old block* I was referring to is Uncle George. Emily's a feisty little thing when she doesn't want help. But other than that, she's doing just fine."

After tightening the cinch, Emily turned to Matt, slapped her hands on her denim-clad hips and grinned. "See? I did it by myself."

"I'm *impressed*."

So was Miranda, but not so much at her daughter's skill when it came to riding the pony, but at the way Matt and Emily seemed to have hit it off so quickly.

"Do you want me to give you a boost into the saddle?" Matt asked.

"Nope." Emily stood as tall as her little girl stature would allow, brushed her hands together, then reached for the pony's reins. "I can do that by myself, too. Just watch me."

An easy grin tugged at Matt's lips, and Miranda let out a soft sigh of relief. She knew better than to think that he'd forgiven her for keeping their daughter a secret from him for so long, but at least he didn't seem nearly as angry as he'd been.

"See how stubborn and insistent she can be," Matt said. "Maybe you should have named her Georgina, after our headstrong, favorite uncle."

"She's a little bullheaded. I'll give you that." But then again, so was her father.

Memories of that handsome young cowboy and days gone by popped up like spring flowers. First love, new life. Stolen kisses while frosting homemade cupcakes. Holding hands while watching TV and munching on popcorn.

What Miranda wouldn't give to roll back the clock and return to that simpler time.

"So," Matt said, drawing her back to the present. "When is your baby due?"

Miranda's heart darn near stopped, and she could hardly take a breath, let alone form a single word. Instead, she continued to lean on the corral for support and turned to him in stunned silence.

"I'm sorry," he said. "That's none of my business."

No, she supposed it wasn't. But that was another secret she couldn't keep from him any longer. "I'm due on September second."

He merely nodded.

"It's a boy," she added.

He glanced at Emily, who galloped her pony inside the corral. "Does she know she's going to have a little brother?"

"I'm sure she'll be thrilled, but I haven't told anyone yet." She expected Matt to address her confession, to offer an opinion, a judgment. Something. But his gaze remained on the child.

About the time she thought he'd dropped the subject completely, he asked, "So your father doesn't know?"

"No, but I plan to call him tomorrow. I'll tell him then."

At that, Matt's focus finally shifted, and he turned to face her, his elbow resting on the corral. His weight shifted to one hip, allowing him to take the burden off his bad knee. "Are you *afraid* to tell him?"

"No, I'm not." She'd been more afraid to tell her dad that she was going to have Matt's baby. Just as she'd expected, when he found out, he'd been more than a little upset. But he'd gotten over his initial anger when he realized he would be a grandfather. And once he'd seen Emily and held her in his arms, he'd made a complete about-face. So Miranda had no reason to expect a different reaction from him this time.

"So what are you waiting for?" Matt's gaze drilled into her, but not in an accusatory or judgmental way. He seemed more curious than anything. And wanting answers.

But she couldn't blame him for that. Her current situation could inspire a new reality TV show: *The Pregnant Runaway Bride*.

"Just to be clear," she said, "I regret ever getting involved with Gavin, but I'm actually happy about having another baby. It's not this little boy's fault that his unexpected arrival has complicated my life. My dad's, too."

"How so?"

"Besides the obvious?" She tucked a strand of hair behind her ear. "I play an active role in the family business."

"It doesn't look like you're doing a very good job of that now."

"You're right. My dad had to hire an accountant from a temp agency to cover for me. From what he told me, things are getting done at the office, but the temporary setup is getting old, and he'd like me to come back."

"He's always had big plans for you," Matt said. "Like graduating from high school as a valedictorian and attending an Ivy League college."

"True." Not to mention getting an accounting degree and eventually running the business he and his father started from the ground up.

"How long do you plan to stay with George on the Double G?" he asked.

"If your uncle doesn't mind, I'd like to stay until after the baby is born. But eventually, I need to find a place of my own, something with some property. Not a ranch, but I'll need room for all of Emily's barnyard friends."

"That's for sure," Matt said, a smile tilting his lips.

Miranda relished his upbeat mood for a couple of beats, wishing it was here to stay, then glanced into the corral, where her daughter—*their* daughter—and Oreo loped in a figure-eight pattern.

The kid was a natural. Was horsemanship genetic? In this case, it certainly seemed to be.

Over the years, Miranda had tried her best to forget her first—and *only*—love and move on, but she'd never been able to. How could she? Every time she looked at their daughter, she was reminded of the cowboy who'd stolen her heart when she was in high school.

And now, seeing the two of them together for the first time was surreal. And heartwarming.

Without a conscious thought, she risked another glance at Matt, and something stirred deep in her soul, something warm and…tender. Special.

Or was it more than that?

Not that Miranda was interested in rekindling an old flame. She knew better than to waste her thoughts on something crazy like that.

Matt might be willing to step up and be a father to Emily. But she couldn't expect him to want to take on a baby who wasn't his.

Chapter Five

As a rumbling engine sounded outside, Miranda glanced out the office window and spotted George returning to the ranch in his old pickup.

As planned, she'd spent the rest of the morning paying the monthly bills and balancing the ledger, a task she'd just completed. So she gathered up the checks George needed to sign and placed them in a stack.

She'd no more than started down the hall, headed to the kitchen to greet him, when George called out, "Chicken's on the table."

Since Emily was probably still outside, Miranda would have to find her and tell her to wash up for lunch. As she entered the kitchen, she expected to see George laying food out on the table, but all she found were several heat-resistant boxes containing the meals he'd brought home.

She suspected he must have gone to tell Matt and Emily it was time to eat, so she proceeded to pull out napkins and paper plates from the pantry.

Her cell phone rang before she could take a step. She glanced at the lighted display. Spotting her father's name, she let out a little sigh, then swiped her finger across the screen of her iPhone and answered. "Hey, Papa. What's up?"

"Everything, it seems. From the moment I woke up, if something could go wrong, it did. I started out the day with a routine dental exam only to end up having a root canal. Then Diego Martinez called. That new farming venture in Mexico is going south, and I need to fly to Los Mochis later this afternoon to straighten things out."

"That's too bad. I'm sorry, but I guess some days are like that."

He sucked in a deep breath and blew out a heavy sigh. "I know you wanted to distance yourself from Gavin. And I don't blame you. But when are you coming home, *mija*? I could sure use someone in my corner right now."

Miranda chewed her bottom lip. She'd planned to tell her father everything tomorrow, after she'd gotten her thoughts in order. Then again, she had him on the phone now.

Just get it over with and put it behind you.

She opened her mouth to speak, but a response shriveled up in her throat like a dried sponge, and her tongue couldn't seem to find any words. The poor guy was having a bad day already, and her news would send him over the edge.

Boy, she could sure use a drink of water. Not to mention a believable excuse. So she crossed the room, cell phone pressed to her ear, and headed for the fridge. "I'm sorry I'm not there for you, Papa, but I'm not quite ready to come back yet."

If truth be told, she wasn't sure she wanted to return at all, other than to pack up her belongings and call a moving van.

"But it's been three months, *mija*. I know you're staying with a friend, but aren't you afraid you'll wear out your welcome?"

She cringed at the reminder of the excuse she'd given him when she'd first told him she needed time away. She was staying with a friend, but she'd led him to believe it was someone she'd met in college.

For a woman who'd always prided herself on being honest, she'd certainly pushed the limits on more than one occasion.

"Besides," Papa said, "the office isn't the same without you."

"I miss you, too." She removed a cold bottle of water from the refrigerator.

As she closed the door and turned away, she noticed a torn wadded-up piece of paper on the floor next to the metal trash can. She picked it up, realizing it had once been a small white bag with a red pharmacy logo, its contents—most likely medication—hastily removed. It hadn't been there this morning. Had Uncle George gone into town to pick up a prescription? That was a little unusual, since she'd never seen him take anything.

"So how're you doing?" her father asked. "And how's Emily? I sure miss my girls."

"We're both having a good time. And Emily couldn't be happier. She loves playing outdoors, especially with my friend's dog, pony and other barnyard critters. I wouldn't be surprised if she decided to become a veterinarian."

"That's great. It won't hurt for her to start thinking about college. But you know I'm not a fan of home-schooling, so I hope that's only going to be temporary, while you're away. I think she'd do better in a regular classroom."

"I agree." That's why Miranda had enrolled her in Brighton Valley Elementary, which was currently on spring break.

"When will you two be home? I don't have anyone to spoil with glazed doughnuts on Sunday mornings."

"I'll bring Emily to see you in a week or two." And she would. That would give her time to tell him about the baby and for him to get used to the idea. But that visit would be brief. She wasn't going to stay in San Antonio any longer than she had to.

"By the way," she asked, "is that accountant from the temp agency still working out?"

"He's okay. He tries hard. But he's not you, *mija*."

Just then the backdoor creaked open. Emily entered the house first, followed by George.

"What kind of chicken did you bring us?" Emily asked.

Miranda's heart slammed into her chest.

"Listen," she said, "I have to hang up, Papa. I'll give you a call in a couple of days."

Then she disconnected the line before he overheard a name or recognized a voice that would unravel her secret before she had a chance to reveal it at a better time.

And in a much better way.

By the time four o'clock rolled around, Matt had built up a powerful thirst, so he went to the kitchen, where he found everyone had gathered. Emily and Miranda were working on a jigsaw puzzle at the table, while George was standing in front of the freezer, filling a glass with ice cubes. Even Sweetie Pie was seated on her haunches, tail thumping the floor, yet eyeing Matt as if she still wasn't convinced he could be trusted.

"We finished off that chicken at lunch," George said. "So how about chili beans for dinner? I've got a couple of cans in the pantry. There should be a box or two of that cornbread mix. But if not, I'm pretty sure we have saltines."

Matt had survived his teen years eating simple fare that didn't require much effort on the cook's part, but canned chili had never sounded very good to him. Besides, he didn't come to the Double G expecting someone to wait on him or to take care of all his needs. "It's my turn, so I'll get dinner tonight."

"All right." George took the jug of sweet tea from the fridge and filled his glass.

"I don't mind cooking," Miranda said. "I can make a run to the grocery store."

"You can do that tomorrow," Matt said, as he fixed himself a glass of tea. After taking a big swig, he made his way over to the table to check out the puzzle, a colorful scene with a fairy tale theme.

Emily looked up and gifted him with a dimpled grin. "Want to help us, Matt?"

He returned her smile. "No, I'll just watch. You two seem to be fine without me."

George took a sip of tea, then asked, "What do you have in mind for dinner, Matt? If you want to grill, there's plenty of meat in the freezer, so it'll need to be thawed. Or you'll have to go to the market. And, come to think of it, we're getting low on propane."

"Let's make this easy. I'll drive into Brighton Valley and order something from Caroline's Diner to go."

"That's a great idea. Simple, tasty and filling." George reached into his back pocket. "And while you're there, check out the desserts. I've got a hankerin' for something sweet, especially if Caroline made it fresh today."

When George withdrew the beat-up leather wallet that had molded to fit his backside, Matt raised the flat of his hand. "Put your money away. I've got it covered."

"All right-y," George said. "Then I won't fight you."

Matt felt a tug on his shirtsleeve and looked down at Emily.

"Can I go with you?" she asked, her soft brown eyes hopeful.

Matt didn't mind taking her, but he glanced at

Miranda, seeking her approval. "You'll have to ask your mom."

Miranda, who'd just removed a puzzle piece that had been placed in the wrong spot, looked up and caught his eye. She didn't respond right away, so he figured she was uneasy about him taking Emily on his own. But why wouldn't she be worried about that? Matt didn't know squat about kids, especially little girls.

After a beat, she asked, "Are you sure you don't mind taking her with you?"

"No," he said, "not at all. You can even go with us. Unless you've got better things to do."

She nodded toward the puzzle, then turned to him and laughed. "Are you kidding? This is the only project I have going on right now, but it can wait until we get back. Give me a minute, and I'll meet you outside."

Matt had learned that, most of the time, when a woman asked for a minute, she took much longer than that, but Miranda surprised him by actually making it quick.

As he opened the truck's rear passenger door to let Emily into the backseat, Miranda came outside wearing a pretty pale green dress and a pair of boots. She'd brushed out her dark brown hair and let the curls tumble over her shoulders. And she'd freshened her lipstick. As she headed toward his pickup with a spring in her step and a breezy smile, she looked more like a woman who belonged on a ranch than a CPA who spent her days working in an office.

He hated to admit it, but he still found her stunningly attractive—with or without the baby bump.

"I haven't been to Caroline's Diner in years," she said, as she climbed into his pickup, filling the cab with a hint of her perfume—something soft and alluring that reminded him of spring flowers. "Has it changed much?"

"Not that I know of," Matt said. "Unless Caroline did some remodeling since I was there the winter before last."

"Does Margie still work there?"

Matt chuckled. "I'm sure she does—unless she landed a job as the gossip columnist at the *Brighton Valley Gazette*. And even then, she'd probably hang out at the diner to pick up the latest news."

"I remember her being a bit nosy and talkative," Miranda said. "But she was very sweet."

"You have her pegged just right. Some people never change." Matt glanced across the seat at his former high school sweetheart. And of course, some did.

Two days ago, he never would have thought he'd see Miranda again, let alone learn that she'd given birth to his daughter. And now look. Here they were, riding together to Caroline's Diner, kicking up dust along the long driveway to the county road and stirring old memories he'd thought that he'd forgotten.

After parking along Brighton Valley's quaint tree-lined Main Street, they climbed out of Matt's pickup and headed to the diner. In spite of the addition of a fancy steak house and the Italian restaurant that opened a couple of years ago, Caroline's was still popular with the locals.

The last time Miranda and Matt had come to Caroline's for a burger and fries, they'd sat in a corner booth, hidden from view, and she'd prayed her father or one of his friends or associates wouldn't spot her. Little had she known that he'd hired a PI to find her, a man who'd followed them inside, then told her father what she'd been up to.

The bell over the diner's door jingled, announcing their entry, but other than two old men seated at the lunch counter, the place was surprisingly empty. Miranda scanned the interior of the familiar eatery, with its pale yellow walls and white café-style curtains on the front windows.

"Look!" Emily pointed to the refrigerator display case that sat next to the old-fashioned register. "Are we going to have dessert tonight? I love chocolate cake."

"You bet," Matt said. "I like chocolate, too. I'll also pick up a lemon meringue pie. That's Uncle George's favorite."

Emily turned away from the desserts long enough to notice the chalkboard where Caroline posted her daily specials.

As usual, she'd written it in yellow chalk: *What the Sheriff Ate—Pork Chops, Mashed Potatoes and Gravy, Buttered Green Beans, Biscuits and Peach Cobbler.*

"What's that mean?" Emily asked, pointing to the board.

"Caroline's husband used to be the sheriff," Miranda explained. "He's retired now, but everyone still refers to him with that title."

"And so he ate pork chops for lunch?" Emily

scrunched her brow. "Why do people need to know that?"

Margie, who was still in the kitchen, must have heard the bell at the door jingle-jangle because she called out, "Y'all don't need to wait to be seated. Take any table you like."

"It's going to take a while for them to get our dinner orders ready," Matt said. "And there's hardly anyone here now, anyway. Let's go ahead and sit down."

When he pointed to a table near the window, Miranda placed her hand on Emily's shoulder, then steered her to the spot he'd selected. She would've preferred that they sit in the corner booth, even though it might provoke memories neither of them ought to poke at. A few of her dad's friends still lived in town, although he probably hadn't kept in touch with them after moving to San Antonio. He ran in a different social circle these days.

Besides, she had every intention of being the one to tell him where she was staying. And she'd do that soon. Very soon.

"This place is funny," Emily said, as she took a seat. "They have bells on their doors, and they tell each other what they eat."

"You're right," Matt said, as he leaned his cane against the wall, then pulled out his chair.

They'd no more than taken their seats when Margie stopped by the table with two adult menus and one for a child, as well as a plastic cup filled with crayons. The instant she recognized Matt, she offered him a bright-eyed grin and winked. "Well, if it isn't our local bull riding champ! Welcome home, cowboy. We're all looking forward to seeing you compete in the Rocking Chair Rodeo."

Matt didn't respond.

When Margie glanced at Miranda, her jaw dropped. "Well, now. Isn't this a nice surprise. I haven't seen you in years."

"It's been a while," Miranda said. "How are you?"

"I'm doing just fine. Thanks for asking." Margie zeroed in on Emily, who was busy checking out the puzzles on her menu and removing a red crayon from the little cup.

"And who is this sweet little thing?" Margie asked.

Emily looked up from her work long enough to offer the waitress a smile, then went back to a word search.

"This is Emily," Miranda said, "my daughter."

"*Our* daughter," Matt corrected.

Margie gasped, and Miranda wanted to slip under the table, although she wasn't sure why. Shouldn't she be glad that Matt had claimed Emily as his child?

"Well, now." Margie studied Emily for a beat, then her eyes twinkled. "Isn't that nice?"

Isn't it? Miranda's life story was about to be blasted on the front page of the *Brighton Valley Gazette*. Thank goodness, she didn't need to use the bathroom—yet. The last thing she needed was for Margie to see her baby bump and jump to conclusions. She shot a glance at Matt, but he didn't seem to be concerned.

"I had no idea you two got married," Margie said. "The last I heard, your daddy didn't approve of Matt."

He probably still didn't, although Miranda knew,

with time, her father would come around. He always did. It's just that he was prone to having knee-jerk reactions at first.

"Miranda and I didn't get married," Matt said, as he placed his hand on Emily's shoulder, a move that appeared awkward until the child looked up at him and smiled. "But we couldn't be happier to share this little girl."

"I can sure see why," Margie said. "She's a real cutie."

"Not only that," Matt added, "she's smart, too. And she has a big heart."

The door swung open, and the bell jingled, announcing that a new customer had just entered. Margie turned toward the front of the diner, offered the entrant a bright-eyed grin and waved. "Come on in, Doc. Take a seat anywhere." Then she returned her attention to Matt. "While you look over the menu, I'll get y'all started with some water."

"Actually," Matt said, "we're going to order four meals to go. And while we're trying to decide what we want to take home, we'll have three slices of that chocolate cake."

"You've got it," Margie said, as she headed for the refrigerator display case at the front of the diner.

"Hey, Rick." Matt waved over the dark-haired man Margie had referred to as Doc. In a flannel shirt, jeans and boots, he didn't look like a doctor. Then again, Matt and his high school buddies all had nicknames, but she'd never met this guy.

"Well, I'll be darned," Rick said, extending a hand

for Matt to shake. "I heard you had a hard ride. How are you doing?"

Matt nodded toward his cane. "All right, I guess. But I'm not getting better as quickly as I'd hoped."

"It takes time to mend, but I'm sure you'll be back to fighting weight in no time."

Matt turned to Miranda, introduced her as an old friend and Emily as his daughter. "This is Doctor Rick Martinez. About five or six years ago, when Doctor Grimes retired, Rick bought his practice."

Miranda had met Dr. Grimes once, when he came out to the Double G to treat Bandit, Matt's prized gelding. He and George were cousins, if she remembered correctly.

"So now Rick is the town veterinarian," Matt added. "And he's a darn good one at that."

Emily set down her crayon and gave the man her full attention. "I'm going to be a veterinarian when I grow up."

"That's awesome," Rick said. "You must be an animal lover like me."

She nodded proudly. "I have a dog, a pony, a lamb and chickens."

"You don't actually *have* those animals," Miranda corrected. "They belong to Uncle George."

Emily clicked her tongue. "Sweetie Pie is mine because I found her, and he said I could have her. And when we move to a new house with a big yard, I get to take them all with us. So they're practically mine already."

Miranda could hardly argue that. And no matter

where she decided to live, she'd never end up back at her condo in San Antonio. They allowed pets, but the landlord would never agree to chickens, a lamb or a pony.

As Emily chattered away, Miranda glanced at Matt, who was smiling as he watched the conversation unfold between Dr. Martinez and their daughter. If Emily decided not to major in veterinary medicine, she should consider a career as an investigative reporter. She certainly appeared to have an aptitude for it.

"Do you operate on animals, too?" Emily asked.

"Whenever I have to. I have a small surgical suite in my clinic, but if my patient is a large animal, like a horse, I refer patients to the equine hospital in Wexler."

Emily scrunched her brow and bit down on her bottom lip, then looked up at Dr. Martinez. "Do you ever operate on chickens?"

A smile tugged at the vet's lips. "Not usually. Why do you ask?"

"Because I have a chicken named Nugget, and she has a crooked toe. I don't know how it happened, but it's been like that ever since we got her. And I think we should fix it for her."

Dr. Martinez stroked his chin, as if giving the medical dilemma some thought. "Can Nugget walk?"

"Yes."

"Does she limp or act like it hurts?"

"No."

"Then I wouldn't recommend surgery. She's adapted just fine."

Miranda liked the doctor already. He seemed to have

an amazing bedside—or rather diner-side—manner, and he was great with kids. Rather than tell Emily that an injured chicken was more likely to end up in a roasting pan than an operating table, he took her questions seriously.

"The other chickens peck at her sometimes," Emily added, "and I think it's because of her toe."

"Chickens have what we call a pecking order. They rank each other, and those on the low end get pecked more often. So whatever their reason for pecking on Nugget, I don't think it has anything to do with her toe."

Emily seemed to think about that for a while.

When the bell attached to the diner door jingled again, Dr. Martinez glanced over his shoulder and waved. "I'll be right with you, boys."

"Is that Lucas?" Matt asked.

"Yep. He's in high school now. I'm meeting him and one of his classmates here to discuss colleges that offer degrees in veterinary medicine."

"Already?" Matt furrowed his brow. "I can't believe Lucas is already thinking about college."

"He's sixteen," Rick said. "And the twins are four."

"They were practically newborns when I saw them last." Matt laughed. "Time flies, huh?"

"You've got that right." Rick nodded toward the teens who were studying the desserts in the refrigerated display case. "I'd better go before they eat up all the good stuff."

"Give Mallory my best," Matt said.

"I'll do that. And if we don't get together before

the rodeo, we'll see you there. I've already purchased our tickets."

As the vet turned away from the table, Matt said, "Hey, Rick. One of these days, I'd like to bring Emily to your clinic for a tour. I'm sure she'd like to see your pet rescue, too."

"Absolutely. You can bring her by anytime. Just give me a call to make sure I'm there and not visiting one of the ranches."

"You got it."

Rick had barely taken two steps when Miranda caught Matt's attention and mouthed, "Thank you."

Matt shrugged a single shoulder, as if he hadn't done anything worthy of her appreciation.

As his gaze fixed on their daughter, a slow smile curved his lips and dimpled his cheeks.

Miranda's heart fluttered to life and beat in a way it hadn't in years. And for a moment, she feared she was falling in love with Matt all over again.

Slow down, she told herself. *And be careful.*

If she let down her guard, she might fall hard. And if that happened, she didn't see things ending any better than they had nine years ago.

Chapter Six

Two days later, Matt sat on the edge of his bed and rubbed his aching knee. He had to admit it felt better, but he was a far cry from being at one hundred percent. And if he wasn't completely healed, that meant he couldn't compete in the Rocking Chair Rodeo, an event where everyone in town expected to see him.

Even if he could pull off climbing on the back of a bull, one more hard fall and bad landing could create a more lasting and permanent injury. And then where would he be?

He got to his feet and limped to the closet, holding the cane rather than using it. Then he slid open the door and placed the cane inside. Maybe, if he wasn't using it anymore, he'd convince himself that he'd be fully recovered soon.

As he stood in the center of the small but comfortable room that had once been his great-grandmother's, he scanned the interior, which hadn't changed in years.

After Matt's dad asked George to let Matt move in and live out his teen years on the Double G, George had purchased the blue-plaid bedspread that covered the bed, replacing the pink-and-beige quilt that his mother had made before she died.

The maple chest of drawers and matching nightstand, probably considered antiques, had once belonged to her, too. But other than that, there wasn't much to remind Matt of the woman he'd never met.

He'd added his own touches to the room—rodeo posters that still adorned the walls, several framed photos that dotted the chest of drawers. He crossed the room and picked up one of him and his buddies; they were wearing their football uniforms—dirt-smudged faces, happy grins and drenched in ice water after winning the division title.

Matt studied the picture of himself, along with Clay "Bullet" Masters and Adam "Poncho" Santiago, and couldn't help but smile. They'd been fun-loving, mischief-prone teenagers back then, and as a result, they were often in trouble at school.

The worst and probably last time any of them crossed a line was when a harmless prank went awry and injured a janitor. Charges were filed, and if Adam's foster dad, a respected police officer, hadn't gone to bat for them, they might have spent some time in juvenile hall. That was the first time Matt had someone defend him, and he'd never forgotten it.

Behind several other pictures, he spotted a photo of him and Miranda, standing next to Bandit, the horse he'd had to put down three months after Miranda left town. That second devastating loss had only made the first one worse.

Matt had been so hurt by Miranda's rejection that he'd been tempted to throw that photo in the trash or burn it or tear it to pieces, just like she'd done to him. But it was the only picture he had of Bandit, so he'd stuck it upside down in the lower dresser drawer instead.

So who'd gone through his things and put that picture back on display? Not that they'd placed it front and center. Still, Matt certainly hadn't done it.

It might've been his uncle, he supposed, but George had always respected Matt's privacy in the past. It didn't seem likely that he'd rummage through his drawers. He supposed it might have been the cleaning woman George hired to come in every couple weeks.

A knock sounded at his door—a loud rap, not one of the soft tentative knocks he'd come to expect from Miranda.

"Come in." He turned away from the photographs and watched George enter the room.

"I've got one of the new hands fixing the pump in the north forty," George said. "He's still a little wet behind the ears, so I need to go out there and supervise. Since you're taking Emily to tour the veterinary clinic today, I wondered if you'd pick up something for me while you're in town and save me a trip."

"Sure. What is it?"

"A prescription at the drugstore. No big deal if you can't. I'll find time to get it later this afternoon."

George rarely visited the doctor. "What's it for?"

"An antibiotic for an infected toenail. Like I said, it's no big deal."

"I'll get it after Emily's tour."

"By the way," George said, "she's waiting outside for you, next to your truck."

"Already? If we go now, we'll show up about twenty minutes early."

George chuckled. "She was so excited, she hardly touched her lunch. I'd say she's eager to get on the road."

"Yeah, I know." He'd figured that out when she darn near talked Rick's ear off at Caroline's Diner. "She's going to like visiting the clinic."

A slow smile slid across George's face. "You're going to be a good father."

"I don't know about that." Matt shrugged a single shoulder. "But I'm going to try. You can't expect more than that from a guy who's never been close to his own dad."

"It won't be hard. Just try to be the kind of man you wished your father would've been."

A man like George, he supposed. And maybe one like Adam's foster dad. Neither of them had had kids of their own, but they'd both stepped up and provided damn good role models for a couple of angry and rebellious teenagers.

"Speaking of fathers," George said, "have you talked to yours lately?"

"Not since I had that run-in with Grave Digger. He called me, but not because he was concerned about my injury. He asked if I could get a couple of VIP tickets for him and my *brother* to attend the Rocking Chair Rodeo." Matt rolled his eyes. "I told him I couldn't."

"Sounds like you're still holding a grudge."

"Shouldn't I?"

George seemed to chew on that for a while, then said, "Family is important. And for the record, I'm glad you're part of mine."

Matt was pretty much George's only relative—other than Matt's dad, who rarely visited him, even on holidays. But hell, why would he do that when he'd chosen his second wife's family over the one he'd had?

"I don't think you call two people a family," Matt said.

"You know what they say about quality over quantity."

"I suppose you're right, but since I got shut out of the only real one I had, I don't have the foggiest idea how to create one, let alone be a part of one."

"You'll figure it out."

He'd have to. Things might have been different if his mom hadn't died when he was too young to remember her, if he hadn't spent so much time with babysitters or in day care. And it would've been a hell of a lot different if his old man hadn't fallen heart over brains for a woman with a kid of her own. But that's how it had all come down, and he'd dealt with it the best way he'd known how.

Matt studied the old man who'd become the only

father he really cared about, the man he'd come to love. "Did you put that picture of me and Miranda on my dresser?"

"You noticed, huh?" George grinned.

"Being snoopy or nosy isn't like you."

George arched a gray brow. "You mad about that?"

"Why shouldn't I be? You went through my drawers."

"I did your laundry the day after you left to follow the damned ol' rodeo. And I figured you weren't quite ready to throw it away, or you would have."

Matt let out a humph and slowly shook his head.

George nodded toward the bedroom doorway. "Like I said, Emily's waiting for you. And I suspect her mother would like to go, too, even if she didn't mention it."

Matt hadn't planned to include Miranda unless she asked. And even then he was reluctant to take her with him.

He might have built a heavy-duty wall around his heart—just ask some of the women who'd thought they'd be able get a commitment out of him.

But that wall had been a lot easier to maintain when Miranda was long gone—and out of sight.

Miranda hadn't asked Matt if she could go with him to the veterinary clinic, even though she really wanted to. Emily was going to enjoy the special tour, and Miranda would have loved to be a part of it. But she didn't want Matt to think that she and Emily were a package deal. And worse, she didn't want him to suspect that she had any romantic notions about starting up where they'd left off. She knew better than that. So she'd returned to the office to do the payroll, even though it was a day early.

She'd barely gotten started when a soft knock against the doorjamb sounded. She looked up from her work and spotted Matt in the open doorway, wearing a sheepish grin.

"I can see that you're pretty busy," he said, "but did you want to go to the clinic with us?"

She tamped down her enthusiasm and said, "Sure. If you don't mind. It sounds like fun. And my office work can wait."

And now here they were, entering a veterinary clinic with their delighted daughter, pretending to be a family, when they were anything but.

While Matt sat in the waiting room, Miranda studied his profile, the blond hair, neatly cut and styled, collar length, but not as wild as he'd worn it nine years ago. His eyes, as blue as the summer sky, were framed with thick dark lashes a woman would die for—pretty lashes their daughter had inherited.

He seemed so different from the guy she'd once loved, yet at the same time, there was a bit of the old Matt in him. And he hadn't shaken that cowboy swagger. If anything, he'd honed it, and she found it sexier than ever.

No wonder women flocked around him, eager to have a chance to spend some time, if not the night, with the champion bull rider.

Miranda rested her hand on her baby bump, which served as a nice reminder for her to keep those old memories at bay, and scanned the waiting room, with its pale green walls and built-in fish tank. She expected Emily to be immediately drawn to the colorful tropical fish. Instead, the girl zeroed in on a gray-haired man seated on one of the brown vinyl chairs and holding a cat carrier, a gray tabby resting inside.

"Can I see your kitty?" she asked him.

"Of course," he said. "Do you like cats?"

"Yes. I like *all* animals." Emily stooped to peer into the carrier. "What's her name?"

"It's a boy. His name is Archie."

"How come he's in a cage? Does he bite?"

"Oh, no. Archie's very friendly. But sometimes, there's a dog or two in the waiting room. And so I bring him in his carrier, where he's safe. He's much happier this way."

"Oh." Emily eased closer to the animal.

Miranda glanced at Matt, saw a grin curling his lips. He seemed to be as proud of their daughter as she was. And as intrigued by her friendly manner.

As if sensing Miranda's assessment, Matt turned to her and smiled. The glimmer in his eyes was that of a proud daddy, but then it shifted, morphing into the kind he used to shine on her. As their gazes locked, her senses reeled and her heart darn near stopped. Old memories popped up, taking her back to the days when things had been different between them. When she and Matt had envisioned a future together.

"Why is Archie here?" Emily asked the cat's owner. "Is he sick?"

"He was, but he's feeling better now. We came in

for a checkup, and we're just waiting to pick up his medicine."

The door to the back office opened, and a woman walked out holding the leash of a German shepherd wearing a plastic cone around its neck.

Emily's interest piqued, and she approached the dog's owner. "What happened to your dog? Why is it wearing that thing?"

The woman, her graying hair pulled up into a top-knot, smiled. "It looks a little silly, doesn't it? But Dr. Rick put this on Sophie to keep her from licking or chewing her stitches."

Before Emily could question the dog owner further, a blonde wearing blue scrubs came to the reception window. "Dennis, here's Archie's prescription. You'll see that Dr. Rick lowered the dose this time."

The older man got to his feet, and with the cat carrier firmly in hand, approached the opening. "Thanks, Kara."

When the door squeaked open again, Rick entered the waiting room and greeted Miranda and Matt. Then he turned to Emily. "Are you ready to check out my clinic and see where I work?"

"Yes!"

"Then let's go." Rick stepped away from the doorway, allowing the child inside, then motioned to Miranda and Matt. "Come on, Mom and Dad."

As the two awkward parents fell into step behind the veterinarian and their daughter, Miranda was tempted to reach for Matt's hand, to pretend they were the family Rick assumed they were.

But she knew better than to rock the boat.

* * *

As they entered the clinic, Matt glanced at Miranda, who mouthed, *Thank you*, as if he'd done her a favor.

He nodded to acknowledge her words, but he hadn't done anything extraordinary. He'd just coordinated a tour for their daughter. Or was she thanking him for including her?

If truth be told, he'd been reluctant to bring her along—and for a slew of reasons. But he couldn't think of a single one of them right now.

"These are the exam rooms," Rick said, pointing out three of them as he led the way through the clinic. Next, he showed them a pharmacy area and a small laboratory, where he let Emily look through a microscope at a blood smear.

Matt glanced at Miranda. Maternal pride glistened in her eyes.

Yeah, he decided. She had been thanking him for including her this afternoon. And in spite of dragging his feet about it earlier, he was glad that he had.

Rick led them to a glass window that provided a view of the operating suite. "If any animals need surgery, this is where it takes place."

They then headed to the boarding area, where several furry patients were recovering or waiting for their owners to pick them up.

"Oh!" Emily said, as she pointed to a cage that housed a mother cat and six nursing kittens. "What's wrong with them?"

"That's Mama Kitty. At least, that's what we're calling her. Kara, my vet tech, found her wandering around in her neighborhood and assumed she was a pregnant stray. The babies were born yesterday. She has a leg wound, which I'm treating. Once it heals, I'll take her to our animal rescue center out back."

"Then what?" Emily asked. "Will they live there forever?"

"No, only until we can find them good homes."

"I have a good home for them." Emily turned to her mother, eyes pleading. "Can we take them back to the ranch and keep them?"

"*All* of them?" Miranda laughed. "I'm afraid not. You've already pushed your limits with poor Uncle George. He's taken in enough strays as it is. And we don't want to wear out our welcome until we find a place of our own."

Did she plan to move to Brighton Valley? Matt wondered. If so, it would put some distance between her and her father, which would be good for her and for Emily. Good for him, too, he supposed. It would make it easier for him to see Emily.

And to see Miranda.

He stole another glimpse at the woman who'd rocked his teenage world. He'd been nineteen and a senior back then. And he'd had his choice of girls. But it was the new girl in school, a pretty dark-haired sophomore, who'd first caught his eye and soon stolen his heart.

Falling for Miranda had really complicated his life back then—in both good ways and bad.

She cast a look his way, caught him gazing at her and blessed him with a pretty smile that could turn a man inside and out. But he shook it off the best he could.

As they continued through the clinic, Rick pointed out his office, with its solid oak desk adorned with antique brass and a Mac computer on top. Then he led them to the back door and took them outside, where a six-foot high chain-link fence encircled a small white house.

"This is the animal rescue yard," Rick said. "I used to live in that house before Mallory and I got married."

Upon their approach, several dogs ran to the fence, barking and wagging their tails.

"You rescue dogs?" Emily asked.

"And cats, rabbits, a goat and, right now, we have a potbellied pig."

The front door of the house swung open, and a balding older man walked out. He squinted, then lifted his hand to block the sun from his eyes and grinned. "Oh. Hi, Doc. I wondered why Scout and Beauty were barking up a storm."

Rick introduced them to the tall, slender man as Roy Dobbins, Kara's grandfather.

"Roy's retired," Rick explained, "so this setup works out well for all of us."

After seeing the dog runs out back, as well as the Kitty Hotel, Matt thanked Rick for showing them around.

"No problem. It was my pleasure."

As they returned to the truck, their shoes crunching on the graveled parking lot, Emily sidled up to him and slipped her hand into his. "That was so awesome. Thank you for bringing me here."

"You're welcome. I was glad to do it. I had a feeling you'd like to see a real veterinary clinic."

She gave his hand a squeeze, then looked up at him with an adoring gaze that shot right through his heart. "You're the best daddy ever."

Matt could have walked on air, had his bum leg not held him back, and he shot a glance at Miranda. Her pretty brown eyes glistened as if she were holding back tears. Happy ones, it would seem, and they touched him in an unexpected way.

For a moment, nothing else in the world seemed to matter. Not her abandonment and his heartbreak. Not an eight-year-old secret she never should've kept. Not even the fact that she was having another man's baby.

Damn. If he wasn't careful, if he let down his guard, she just might complicate his life all over again.

Chapter Seven

As Matt backed out of the clinic parking lot, Miranda settled into the passenger seat feeling a lot more comfortable and at ease than she had when they'd started out.

"Thank you," she said.

Matt shot a glance across the seat. "No problem. I knew Emily would enjoy it. And that she'd learn a lot."

"I did!" Emily said. "That was the best field trip ever."

Miranda waited a beat, then explained what she'd actually been thanking him for. "You didn't have to include me, but I'm glad you did."

"Yeah, well…" He shrugged. "You're welcome."

As he shifted the truck into Drive, Miranda added, "Rick is a great guy, and he clearly loves his work."

"That's true." Matt turned to the left, instead of turning right onto the road, which would have taken them home. "I hope you don't mind, but Uncle George asked me to pick up a prescription for him at the pharmacy."

"Another one?" Miranda asked. "That's odd."

"Why do you find that so unusual?"

"I suppose it's not, but George always told me that he rarely goes to the doctor. Besides, a few days ago, I found a discarded white pharmacy bag. So I'm pretty sure this is a second prescription. Unless it was yours."

"It wasn't mine."

Miranda furrowed her brow. "I hope he's not sick."

"No," Matt said. "He has an ingrown toenail that's infected."

Men like George didn't often take care of themselves. Or seek medical attention. So if his toe bothered him enough to see the doctor, it might be more serious than he'd let on.

She thought about voicing her concern, but decided to confront George instead.

Minutes later, Matt pulled down Brighton Valley's tree-shaded main drag and parked in a space near the pharmacy, which was located a couple doors down from Caroline's Diner.

"It won't take me very long," Matt said. "You guys can wait in the truck if you want to. But if you come inside with me, I'll buy you an ice-cream cone."

"*I'll* come in with you," Emily said. "I *love* ice cream."

So did Miranda. She hadn't visited the old-style

pharmacy since she'd been a teenager. In fact, she and a girlfriend had been eating French fries and drinking cherry colas when Matt first approached her and asked to sit beside them at the counter. Both girls had plans to meet a couple of their classmates for a study group at the library, and it was almost time for them to go. But when Miranda looked into those gorgeous blue eyes, when she saw that dimpled grin, she'd opted to stay behind.

"Do they still have that soda fountain along the side wall?" she asked Matt.

"They sure do. The tourists and the locals would throw a fit if they didn't. But I don't think they offer food or fountain drinks anymore. Both the cook and the woman who used to work behind the counter retired, and the owner hasn't been able to find a replacement."

"That's too bad."

"They still serve ice cream, though. And it's just as good as you remember."

After getting out of the pickup, they entered the charming old pharmacy that had maintained its 1950s style while offering all the latest products and medications. Miranda took a deep whiff, relishing the familiar scent of sweet vanilla laced with something clean and medicinal.

Matt nodded toward the counter that ran along the wall. "Why don't you two have a seat while I pick up George's prescription?"

Miranda steered Emily toward one of the red vinyl upholstered swivel seats that sat in front of the long white counter. "You're going to love this, honey. This was one of my favorite things to do when I used to live in Brighton Valley with your grandfather."

"It's too bad you had to move away from here," Emily said. "Brighton Valley is a fun place to live. I like it a lot better than San Antonio."

So did Miranda. There was a lot to like about the small town, and it hadn't been her idea to leave. She stole a peek at Matt who stood in line, waiting to speak to the pharmacist. She couldn't help admiring the way the sexy cowboy leaned into the counter, the way he'd tilted his hat.

As much as she'd have liked to put Matt at the top of her list of reasons to stick around in town permanently—or at least indefinitely—she knew better than to let him sway her decision. In four short months, she'd be a single mother of two. And he'd still be a handsome rodeo star with his choice of women; a fun-loving man who was always ready to throw back a beer or to circle the dance floor, two-stepping the night away.

But if he wanted a relationship with Emily, which seemed to be apparent, it might be best if she did move back to Brighton Valley—or at least to the general vicinity.

But what would her father say when she told him she wanted to work from home, that she would rarely come to the office in San Antonio?

There's no way he'd agree. She'd heard his speech enough times to recite it verbatim. Mija, *my dad came to the United States as a young man with only the clothes on his back and a gunnysack carrying his few belongs. He had guts and grit and* ganas—desire. He *wasn't educated, so he worked in the berry fields. But he was bright. He learned the ins and outs of farming, literally from the ground up. And by the time I graduated from high school, he'd saved enough to send me, his only son, to college.*

Miranda remembered her grandfather, an older man with sun-ravaged skin, stooped shoulders and a warm smile. A man her papa loved and respected.

As a tribute to my papa, I excelled and received an agriculture degree with a business minor. And then I went home, where my father and I worked and saved so we could purchase enough fertile acreage to plant berries. Together, we built our business for you, mija. *And one day, it'll all be yours.*

Miranda blew out a soft sigh. How could she dash a dream that had carried the Contreras family through two generations?

Before she could ponder the answer, Matt returned to the counter. "The pharmacist is sending the stock clerk over to serve us."

"This place used to be a big tourist draw back in the day," Miranda said. "I remember when they served food here. They had these really cool plastic menus that offered hot dogs, burgers and fries."

"They still have them, although they don't use them anymore." Matt slipped around to the back of the counter and found where a couple of old menus had been stored. He handed one to Emily, then took a seat next to her, placing the child between them. Whether she was a wall or a connection was left to be seen.

Miranda scanned the nostalgic setting. "I imagine it would still be a big draw."

"You're right." Matt looked over Emily's head, which was bent so she could study the menu, his gaze on Miranda. "But Ron Jorgenson, the original owner, passed away a few years back, leaving it to his wife Hazel. His death was unexpected, and Hazel took it hard. The manager has been running things, so I have a feeling Hazel has lost interest."

"For a guy who's been away a lot and on the rodeo circuit, you seem to know a lot about what's going on in Brighton Valley."

"I stay in contact with Bullet and Poncho, who keep me updated. My info comes from a cop and a Life Flight pilot, so it's pretty solid."

"Hmm." She tossed him a playful smile. "So in some ways, you're able to keep your ear out for local gossip—like Margie at the diner."

"Whoa!" He lifted his index finger and moved it back and forth, like a windshield wiper. Yet, a glimmer in his eye told her he'd taken her teasing for what it was. "I wouldn't go that far. I like being in the know, but I'm discreet. My buddies know that I can be trusted not to spread gossip."

"Hey, y'all," a teenage boy said, as he approached the counter. "My name's Danny. What can I get you?"

"We'd like ice-cream cones, unless you still have banana splits." Matt nodded his head at Miranda and winked.

Talk about nostalgia and memories… She and Matt had shared a banana split at this very counter that first day, and he'd taught her how to tie a cherry stem in her mouth—without using her hands.

"We don't have any bananas, whipped cream or cherries," Danny said, "but I have chocolate sauce."

What a shame. Miranda had been prepared to show Matt that she still remembered how to do that amazing trick.

"Sounds like we'd better stick with three cones," Matt said.

At that, Emily looked up and grinned. "What flavors do you have?"

"Chocolate, vanilla, strawberry and black cherry. We can give you different flavor combinations if you order a double or triple scoop."

After they placed their orders, Danny got to work making their cones.

"I was talking to the pharmacist," Matt said, "and he told me they've lost a lot of business to that big super pharmacy that opened up on the border between Brighton Valley and Wexler."

"That's too bad. This place has an amazing small town appeal. Their customers like having the personal attention they can't get at one of the big chain stores."

"I agree. I'd hate to see it go."

Miranda again scanned the setting, then placed an elbow on the counter and turned to Matt. "You know, it might turn out to be a moneymaker and a good investment if Hazel refurbished it."

"Maybe. But I'm not sure if she'd be interested in doing anything other than selling it outright."

Danny handed Emily a strawberry cone, the top scoop tilted slightly off center. "Here you go."

Emily thanked him, then began to lick the side.

As Danny returned to make the other two cones, Matt said, "From what I heard, the woman who used to manage the soda fountain retired."

"And the one before that got pregnant with triplets," Danny added. "For some reason, people who work at the counter keep leaving. My friends and I call it The Curse of the Drug Store Soda Jerks."

"What happened to them?" Emily asked, her lips parted, her eyes open wide.

"They didn't die or anything." Danny carried a single-dip black cherry cone and handed it to Miranda.

"I don't believe in curses," Matt said. "People don't always stick with a job that doesn't pay a lot. But I have to admit, it's kind of weird. About forty years ago, Uncle George dated a woman who worked here. And she not only quit her job, she broke up with him and left him high and dry."

"Why'd she leave?" Miranda asked.

"She ran off with a musician bound for Nashville, and it really messed up George. He's sworn off women ever since—at least, when it comes to romance."

"Poor George." So that's why the man had never married. Miranda nibbled at her cone, then turned to Matt, caught a glimpse of his profile, saw his eye twitch.

He didn't say it, but he didn't need to. Miranda had run off, too.

As Danny handed Matt a double-deck chocolate

cone, Emily got off her swivel seat. "Can I look around the store?"

"I suppose." Miranda could see why the child would be curious. "But don't touch anything."

"I won't."

As Emily stepped away, leaving the two adults at the counter, Miranda made a quarter-spin in her swivel seat and turned to Matt.

"I had a good reason for leaving," she said, her voice soft, hesitant.

He zeroed in on her for a couple of beats, then broke eye contact to study his chocolate cone. "It doesn't matter."

Actually, it did. To her, anyway. And while she felt compelled to insist that he listen, Emily chose that moment to approach a display of colorful refrigerator magnets that was only a few steps away and within earshot.

So it wasn't the time for Miranda to either defend herself or to apologize for breaking his heart.

The afternoon they'd spent at Rick's clinic had turned out even better than Matt hoped it would. And they topped off the day with a simple but filling dinner Miranda had fixed them.

While they munched on baked chicken, rice pilaf and a tossed salad, the adults remained quiet, but mostly because Emily chattered up a storm, rehashing the things she'd seen and learned on her tour and sharing her plans to open her own veterinary hospital and rescue center someday.

Needless to say, no one else had been able to get

a word in edgewise. And that was just as well. Matt hadn't known what to say anyway. Spending time as a family had been pretty surreal.

His mom had died when he was in kindergarten, and since his dad's job required him to travel, Matt had spent a lot of time with babysitters or else he'd been placed in day care for hours on end. Then, when his stepmother and her son had eventually come into his life, she rarely included Matt in those kinds of activities. And that often left Matt alone.

"It's my turn to clean up," George said, as he got up from the table.

Matt didn't argue. Instead, he poured a cup of decaf and slipped out the front door, where he took a seat in one of the rocking chairs.

He'd no more than taken a couple of sips when Miranda opened the screen door and stepped into the soft yellow glow of the porch light.

"There you are." She smiled sheepishly, then tucked a strand of hair behind her ear. "Is it okay if I join you for a few minutes?"

You'd think that he'd resent having an interruption to his solitude, but for some reason, it didn't seem to bother him a bit. "Sure, go ahead."

She took a seat in the rocker next to his. "It's nice outside this evening."

That's why he'd come out here. Well, there was that. But he'd also wanted some time to think. About life. About parenthood.

About *her*.

"I really appreciate how kind you've been to Emily," she said.

How could he not be? He was her father. "She's an amazing kid."

Matt would never turn away from Emily, like his old man and his stepmom had done when they'd both favored her bratty kid over Matt.

Much to his stepmom's aggravation, the house became a battlefield, with Matt getting into trouble for starting the fights even when he wasn't to blame.

His father traveled on business and was gone most of the time, which was nothing new. But each night, when his old man called home, his stepmom would complain about Matt picking on her son or giving her a hard time. You'd think the guy would have at least listened to Matt's side of the story, but he hadn't. And by the time Matt was fourteen, his dad had gotten tired of hearing about every little thing he'd done wrong and shipped him off to live with Uncle George.

But hey. Things had worked out. And in time, Matt had put it all behind him.

He stole a glance at Miranda, who peered up at the sky. He assumed she'd come out here to talk to him, so he waited for her to broach whatever she had on her mind. But she continued to sit in silence.

Apparently, like him, she'd only come outside to enjoy the peaceful sights and sounds of the ranch at night. So he leaned back in his seat and took a deep breath of night air, picking up the ever so soft scent of night-blooming jasmine, listening to the evening breeze rustling the leaves in the maple tree and watching the occasional cloud hide the waning moon as it moved across the starlit sky.

"I enjoyed getting to know Rick a little better," Miranda finally said. "He's a great guy."

"You'll like his wife, too. Mallory is a social worker at the Brighton Valley Medical Center."

Miranda set her rocker in motion, the chair runners creaking against the wood-slatted floor. She seemed especially pensive tonight. When she looked out into the distance and bit down on her bottom lip, he realized that she actually did have something on her mind, something she found difficult to say.

"What's bothering you?" he asked.

She took a deep breath and slowly let it out. "When I called everyone in for dinner this evening, your uncle came in a bit winded. Did you notice?"

Now that she'd mentioned it… "Yes, but he'd been outside and had probably hurried to the house. He always used to fuss when I came in late at mealtime."

"That's possible, I guess."

Her concern for Uncle George didn't surprise Matt. Back in the day, the polished college-bound teen and the gruff old rancher had grown surprisingly close. In fact, his uncle had really taken a shine to her. He'd claimed that was because she kept Matt out of trouble. But it was more than that. George had never married or had kids, and having Miranda around seemed to make them a family.

You be good to that little gal, George had once told him. *She's got a sweet disposition and a great sense of humor. But she's also got a good heart.*

And more than once, after Matt's recent arrival at the Double G, when he'd seen the two of them together, George's words had again rung in his ears: *If I'd had a daughter, I would have wanted her to be just like Miranda.*

And Miranda had felt the same way about him. *I love your uncle. He might have a rough exterior, but he's a real softy, too. Don't get me wrong, I'm close to my father, but sometimes George is a lot easier for me to talk to.*

Miranda stopped rocking and turned her head toward Matt. "I don't doubt that he has an infected toenail, but I haven't seen him limp or heard him complain."

"You think he lied to me when he claimed that prescription I picked up for him was an antibiotic?"

"I don't know. It's just that…" She let out a soft sigh. "I think he's having some health issues… Maybe his heart. Or possibly his lungs."

At that, Matt stiffened. "What makes you say that?"

"He's obviously seen a doctor recently. And he's had two different prescriptions. Would they both be for his toe?"

"Maybe."

"I also caught him stroking his left arm the other day. So when he seemed to have trouble catching his breath this evening…? It's probably nothing, but I'm a little concerned."

Matt hadn't noticed anything unusual, but it had been a long time since he'd been home, let alone spent any quality time with his uncle. Once he went back on the circuit, he'd have to make a point of coming around more often. That is, *if* he went back.

"You know," Matt said, "if he's actually having health issues, I don't think he'd ever admit it. Maybe I should talk to his doctor."

"You won't find out anything by talking to his doctor. The HIPAA regulations won't allow him or her to discuss your uncle's health with you."

"Then I'll just have to ask George and not settle for a *nothing's wrong* answer." Hopefully, if there was anything to be alarmed about, the feisty old codger would open up and level with him.

"Good." Miranda set the rocker in motion again, as if that was settled, but then she looked into the darkness again and began to nibble on her bottom lip.

"What else is bothering you?" he asked.

She didn't respond right away, either to admit or deny it. After a few creaks of the rocker, she stopped the motion completely and turned to him. "I've tried to tell you several times why I left town."

"And I've told you it doesn't matter." Her father had had a strong hold on her back then—and he probably still did. "You were a minor. You had to do what you were told."

Even though she'd returned to the ranch, which showed that she'd grown up and had more gumption, she still hadn't told her father where she was. Nor had she revealed her pregnancy.

"Do you remember that trouble you and your friends got into at the beginning of your senior year?" Miranda asked.

How could he forget? They'd tried to play a trick on the football team, but it backfired and the janitor was seriously injured.

"You were on probation," she added.

And he'd been damned lucky, too. If Poncho's foster dad hadn't gone to bat for them, they could have faced time in juvenile hall or in jail.

"And remember that day things blew up?" she asked.

"When your dad showed up at the ranch?" What a disastrous day that had been. They'd been making homemade ice cream with an old hand-cranking machine on the front porch when her father had arrived, along with a private investigator. Her old man had pitched a real fit.

Matt had tried to tell the berry king that he was in love with his daughter, that he'd never hurt her, but that only seemed to make things worse.

I don't know what kind of picture you've painted for Miranda, Carlos Contreras had said, *but I'm not about to let my daughter waste her life by hooking up with a footloose cowboy hell-bent on trouble. She's destined for bigger and better things.*

Matt had expected Miranda to object, to stand up to her father, to defend their relationship, but she'd buckled instead and had gone home with him.

It had been a crushing and demoralizing confrontation, and in the midst of his anger and resentment, Matt realized that, even if he didn't understand why, Miranda loved and respected her father. So, for that reason alone, he'd been determined to win the guy over, although he hadn't had a clue where to even start.

Matt chuffed. And how had that wild plan worked out?

"When we got home," Miranda said, "my dad accused me of…"

She didn't have to say it. Matt had a pretty good idea what Mr. Contreras had said.

Miranda cleared her throat, then continued with the story that he'd already pieced together on his own. "I swore up and down that we'd never slept together. He eventually believed me and mellowed out some. That's when I called you and suggested that we take a break from each other. And you agreed."

Matt hadn't had any choice other than to go along with the decision her father had made and forced onto her. So he didn't call her for a few days, thinking her father would chill and that he'd talk to her at school. But she never returned to Brighton Valley High. Nor had she called him again.

Later, he found out that she'd left town, and no one would tell him where she went, leaving Matt feeling abandoned yet again.

Miranda might think she'd had a good reason for leaving without a trace. And she probably thought he understood. In a way, he supposed he did, but it was too late to go back in time. Too much had happened. Too much had changed. Yet, one thing hadn't.

He stole a glance at her and saw the way she bit down on her lip, the crease in her pretty brow. He could have reached out to her, taken her hand, given it a forgiving squeeze. Because, in a way, he did forgive her. At least, his anger and resentment had eased. But she'd always be her father's princess, under his wing and under his thumb.

Matt was no longer a *footloose cowboy hell-bent on trouble*, but he doubted that made any difference. The berry king wouldn't find a broken-down bull rider any better suited for his princess.

So he fought the urge to say or do something stupid. Instead, he let Miranda continue with her confession and the apology he couldn't quite accept.

Miranda had no idea whether her words were having any effect on Matt or not, but it helped her to unload the guilt and the painful memories that had plagued her for the past nine years.

"In order to keep us apart," she continued, "my dad pulled me out of Brighton Valley High and sent me back to the private school I used to attend."

"His plan certainly worked. I never saw you after that."

"True. And things only got worse. When I got nauseous several mornings in a row, he realized I was pregnant and that I'd lied to him." Miranda closed her eyes, hoping to blink back the memory, but it didn't work.

Her father narrowed his eyes, scoffed at her and spat out the most hurtful words she'd ever heard. *Apparently, rotten apples don't fall too far from the tree.*

He hadn't actually called her a tramp, but she'd known what he'd meant. Her mother had left them both for another man, a wealthy and influential oil-man. The loss and rejection had hit her dad hard, and he'd never quite recovered from it.

On the other hand, Miranda had only been a baby at the time, so it hadn't really affected her. At least, not directly.

Still, the hateful accusation had cut her to the quick. She might have turned on him right then and there, raised her own ruckus and stood her ground. But what he'd said next nearly knocked her to her knees.

That damned kid is nineteen, and you're seven-teen—which means you're underage. Stay away from him, or I'll call the sheriff.

Miranda sucked in a lungful of the cool night air, then slowly let it out and pressed on. "He threatened to have you charged with statutory rape. And since you were already on probation, I was afraid you'd end up serving time in jail." She looked at Matt, awaiting his reaction, but he merely sat there, stone-faced. Had he even been listening?

She would have gone on, but when he furrowed his brow, considering what she'd told him and possibly pondering his response, the words stalled in her throat.

Finally, he said, "So that's why you left without looking back."

That wasn't true. She'd looked back nearly every day since. She just hadn't contacted him.

"I was willing to do anything to protect you," she added, "so I agreed to never see you again. That's why I stopped calling."

Matt's gaze zeroed in on her. "Okay. I got that. It

was over between us. But you should have told me about the baby."

"Yes, I should have, but I knew what you'd do. If I'd told you I was pregnant, you would have challenged my dad. And then he would have followed through on his threat. So I agreed to live with his aunt in Brownsville and have the baby there."

His silence chilled the night air, and she gripped the rocker's armrests until her fingers ached, waiting for his understanding, if not his forgiveness.

"I can understand why you did what you did," he said. "Back then, anyway. But you're an adult now, and you're still afraid to cross him."

In some ways, she supposed, Matt was right. But these days, when she complied, it was by choice. "I challenge him when I have to."

"Like *when*?"

"The first time was when he called me at my aunt's house and told me that he'd talked to an adoption agency. When I refused to even consider it, he threatened to disown me if I didn't give up the baby and go to college as planned. But I never would have done that, no matter what the consequences."

"That was only a threat. He wouldn't have disowned you. He loves you too much."

"I know." At least, she knew it now. But at the time, after he'd compared her to her mother, she hadn't been so sure.

"So," Matt said, "your dad apparently softened his stance when it came to adoption. You kept Emily, and you went to college."

"That's true, but I threw a fit of my own when he suggested I go to a four-year university and move into a dorm. He actually thought I'd leave Emily with him and let a nanny raise her. But I refused. I went to a local junior college part-time, and eventually, when she was old enough to attend preschool, I transferred to Rice University."

The stifling silence returned, and Miranda pondered the past and the various choices she'd made—both good and bad. She suspected Matt might be doing the same thing.

"I realize you must resent my father," she said, "and under the circumstances, I can't blame you for having hard feelings or even hating him. But he absolutely adores Emily and has apologized a hundred times over for even suggesting I give her up."

Matt chuffed. "You still should have called me—at least once. It's been nine freakin' years, Miranda."

"After she was born, I *did* call, and George told me you'd gone out on the rodeo circuit. He and I talked a bit, but I didn't tell him about Emily."

"You could have asked him to contact me."

She'd thought about it. But news like that should be given face-to-face. "He asked if I wanted to leave a message, but I told him I'd call back after the rodeo season ended."

"But you didn't."

No, not after she'd done an internet search and then scanned various social media sites. She'd learned that Matt was whooping it up with the other cowboys and countless rodeo groupies. But even if she hadn't gotten a glimpse of what his new life was like, she wouldn't have followed him from arena to arena with a newborn.

"I'm sorry, Matt. I should have contacted you. But with each day that passed, the harder it got. Still, I wasn't going to keep it a secret. I planned to tell you about her eventually."

And that time had finally arrived.

She glanced his way, but he continued to look out into the night at the darkened ranch. Had he even begun to understand why she'd stayed away? Would he accept her apology? And more importantly, would he truly forgive her?

"I guess that's all in the past now," he said, without looking at her. "So it doesn't really matter."

But his feelings *did* matter. Call it young love or just a teenage crush from which she'd never recovered, she still cared for Matt, a lot more than she cared to admit. And if he still had any feelings left for her, it would help them co-parent their daughter, assuming he wanted to be that involved in her life.

"So now what?" he asked, as if filing away her excuses, along with her apology.

"I'm not sure." She hadn't gotten that far yet. But maybe he had an answer, a suggestion.

She turned to him, only to find him looking at her. His gaze was intense, but she couldn't spot any lingering anger. He continued to study her in silence, setting off a tingle in her chest, jump-starting her heart once again and sparking a dream she'd once had. A hopeless dream she'd been dodging since the day he arrived at the ranch.

But their lives, their careers, had gone in completely different directions. And the last thing Matt would be interested in was a woman who was pregnant with an-other man's baby, a single mom who'd be opposed to fre-quenting cowboy bars and spending nights on the town.

"I hope we can put this behind us and move on," she said. "For Emily's sake."

"It'll take time, but we probably can."

She let out the breath she'd been holding. "Thanks, Matt."

He continued to eye her, assessing her. Judging her?

She might have looked away, if his expression hadn't softened to the point that it seemed almost…hopeful.

"Matt!" George called from inside the house. "Your cell phone is ringing."

He didn't respond right away. Not to his uncle, not to her. After a beat, he nodded toward the front door. "I'd better get that."

Then he broke eye contact, as well as the frail, tenta-tive connection they'd briefly shared, setting her adrift on uncertainty as she tried to avoid a slew of bobbing memories and emotions.

She watched him rise from the rocker, using the armrests as a brace. He moved with pride and strength, yet at the same time, he seemed vulnerable, and her heart went out to him.

As he took a step, his knee buckled and he listed to the side. She jumped from her seat and reached out to steady him. Her attempt worked, and he straightened.

His gaze met hers again, locking her in place. He didn't thank her. Nor did he move.

She didn't move, either. She didn't even dare to breathe.

Her brain tried to make sense of the silent words he spoke, the memories his touch provoked, only to fail miserably. But for some crazy reason, her heart didn't have that same problem.

In spite of herself, she placed her hand on his jaw, felt the light bristles of his cheek. And against all common sense, she drew his mouth to hers.

Chapter Eight

The second Miranda's hand slipped behind Matt's neck, her fingers lit his skin on fire. And when her lips met his, he was toast. His knees went weak, and his heart began to pump as if there were no tomorrow. And right now, there didn't seem to be any yesterdays, either.

The kiss started soft and tentative, but within a beat, it damn near exploded with pent-up desire and pumped up a demanding erection.

Before he knew it, he'd morphed back into that same stupid kid who'd yet to be hurt, disappointed and abandoned. And that kid only knew one thing. He'd missed Miranda something fierce. And he'd missed *this*.

Her mouth opened, and his tongue slid inside, where it met hers in a heated rush, twisting, tasting. He remembered how good it had been between them, how good it still was.

It was also crazy. What in the hell was he thinking? Kissing Miranda had to be the dumbest thing he'd ever done. Yet, he couldn't seem to help himself from pulling her close and holding her tight.

Her baby bump pressed into him, but even that didn't slow him down. Nor did it matter, as the years rolled away, taking the pain and anger with them and leaving him with this one magical moment in time.

Only the screen door creaking open brought him back to his senses, and he would've jumped a foot—if he hadn't had a bum knee—taking a startled Miranda with him.

"Whoopsy-daisy." George cleared his throat and chuckled. "You missed a call, so I thought I'd bring your phone out to you. But I guess I should've let the damn thing ring."

Matt didn't have the foggiest clue what to say, let alone how to explain this. Not to his uncle, and certainly not to himself.

He took the phone from George and thanked him, his voice thick with guilt and embarrassment and who knew what else.

George was still chuckling to himself as he returned to the house, allowing the screen door to slam behind him.

Matt wished he could do the same thing—slip away, disappear, forget what had just happened under the amber glow of the porch light. But it wasn't the light that had cast a spell on him tonight.

"I'm sorry," he said. But hell, why should he be contrite when she's the one who'd started it?

"Me, too." Her words came out soft and tender. Maybe even fragile.

"I…uh…" He lifted his cell phone to show her a plausible excuse for taking off without addressing what they'd just done, which would only open up a slew of emotion and pain he'd rather not wade through. "I've got a call to return."

"And I have a bedtime story to read." She smiled, then headed indoors, leaving him in one hell of a quandary.

He remained outside for a while, holding his phone, bewildered and kicking himself until his erection subsided.

Finally, he glanced at the lighted screen and saw that his buddy, Clay Masters, had called. If Clay wasn't married and the daddy to twins, which kept him and his wife both busy in the evenings, Matt might have suggested they meet at the Stagecoach Inn that very night for a beer. He could really use a friend right now. He needed someone to talk to.

Not about Miranda, though. His feelings were too convoluted to even think about putting them into words.

No, he was more concerned about his slow recovery—and what that might mean. And who better to open up to than a man who'd suffered an injury that had ended his military career?

Realizing they didn't need to go to the local cowboy

bar and throw back a couple of beers to have a conversation like that, Matt returned Clay's call.

"Hey," his buddy said, "what'd you do, lose your phone?"

"Nope. Just didn't hear it ring. What's up?"

"Not much. I hadn't heard from you in a while and thought I'd touch base. I finally have a little more time on my hands these days. And more energy since the babies are finally sleeping through the night."

Clay and his wife Erica were the proud parents of twins—a boy and a girl—which kept them busy.

"I'm glad you can finally get some sleep at night," Matt said. "That's got to be a relief."

"Yeah, life is finally settling down, In fact, Drew and Lainie are going to watch the twins for us on Saturday night so I can take Erica to a movie and dinner."

Drew Madison, the promotional guru Matt worked with at Esteban Enterprises, had married Erica's twin sister. The couple had recently adopted three little boys—brothers who'd been separated in foster care.

"Since Drew and Lainie have kids now and one on the way," Clay added, "we're going to babysit for each other once a week so we can have date nights."

"That's a great idea."

"The reason I called," Clay said, "is to check in on you. How are you doing?"

"Not as good as I'd hoped. I thought coming home to the Double G would make it easier for me to take it easy and to heal, but that's not working out as well as I'd hoped it would. To tell the truth, I'm a little worried about the slow recovery."

"I know what you mean. I eventually healed from my injury, but I had to make a career change. And that actually turned out okay. I'm a lot happier than I thought I'd be."

"Say," Matt said, "as a Life Flight pilot, you work with a lot of paramedics and probably run across medical professionals all the time. Can you ask around and get the name of a good orthopedic surgeon? I think I should get a second opinion."

"I don't need to. Call Brighton Valley Orthopedics and ask to see Jamal Hillman. One of the guys I work with was involved in a serious car accident and really did a number on his ankle. I thought for sure he'd be permanently disabled, and so did he. But he's coming along great. He's still moving slowly and seeing a physical therapist, but he raves about Dr. Hillman."

"I'll call and make an appointment tomorrow. Thanks."

"No problem, buddy. Keep me posted."

Matt almost mentioned Miranda, but that might lead to questions about how he felt about her, and he really didn't know. Even if he was foolish enough to think that something might eventually develop between the two of them, he certainly wasn't going to do a damned thing about it until he was back to fighting weight and on top of his game.

But keeping Miranda a secret meant he couldn't tell his buddy about Emily, either, which was too bad. The two men had something else in common these days, now that they were both family men.

So, for now, he let it all slide and ended the call on a happier note.

Matt would have plenty of time to tell Clay about all the changes going on in his life, starting with Miranda's arrival. But he had to make an appointment to see Dr. Hillman first. Then again, something told him he might need a miracle, rather than just a second opinion. If he wasn't a champion bull rider, then who was he?

He certainly wouldn't be a man her father would consider good enough for Miranda. And Matt had no intention of facing Carlos Contreras until he was all that and more.

Matt managed to avoid Miranda for the rest of the evening and the following morning. The last thing he wanted was for her to think that kiss meant anything, especially since he had no idea what to tell her.

So after having only coffee for breakfast, which he took outside to drink, he waited until nine o'clock and called Brighton Valley Orthopedics to make an appointment with Jamal Hillman, the surgeon Clay had recommended.

The sooner Matt saw the doctor and got a better idea of what lay in front of him, of what he could expect in the future, the better off he'd be.

Unfortunately, the first available appointment he could get was on Friday afternoon, and that was only because the receptionist was a big rodeo fan and had squeezed him in.

"Come early," she said. "And expect to wait."

That meant avoiding Miranda for another four days,

which wouldn't be easy. So he told George he had an out-of-town meeting with the Rocking Chair Rodeo promoters, then checked into the Night Owl Motel and tried to keep a low profile.

Talk about going to extremes.

By the time Friday rolled around, Matt was more than ready to get his life back on track. At the very least, he'd be happy just to get a good night's sleep in his own bed.

Now he was seated in the waiting room at Brighton Valley Orthopedics, holding a magazine he was too antsy to read and listening for his name to be called.

Minutes later, a matronly brunette wearing pale blue scrubs called out, "Matt Grimes?"

He set aside the *Field and Stream* and made his way to the open doorway that led to the back office.

Once he'd been asked to take a seat on an exam table, he waited another fourteen minutes until a tall young doctor wearing neatly styled dreadlocks entered the room introducing himself as Dr. Hillman and offering Matt a friendly smile and a firm professional handshake.

"Tell me about your injury," the doctor said.

Matt explained how it had happened and what the previous doctor had told him. Then he handed over the digital X-rays he'd been given.

Dr. Hillman studied them, then said, "The bone isn't fractured, although I see what could be a small crack in one of the inner bones."

That was news to Matt. Apparently, someone hadn't noticed that before.

The doctor turned away from the black-and-white image and probed Matt's knee. "It's still pretty swollen."

"The initial pain has eased up some, but at times, it still hurts like hell."

"I'd like to take another X-ray," the doctor said.

"To find out if it's healing?"

"Yes," Dr. Hillman said, "but I'd also like to see if there've been any new developments that have made things worse. I'm also going to order an MRI to see the extent of the tissue damage, and we may want to follow that up with an ultrasound."

Matt had always been leery of people in the medical field, but something told him that he was in good hands now.

"We can do it all in this office," Dr. Hillman added, "but we're a little behind today, so you'll have to wait until the tech is free."

"No problem. I don't have anything pressing to do. I just want this thing to heal. And the sooner the better."

An hour later, Matt had finished getting both the X-ray and the MRI, both of which he'd been told would be digital images. That, in itself, suggested Brighton Valley Orthopedics had a state-of-the-art operation.

Now he was back in the waiting room, thumbing through another magazine he couldn't quite get into. As much as he would've liked to complain about all the time this was taking, he realized he was partly to blame for the heavy schedule and kept his mouth shut.

Finally, a different woman wearing pink scrubs called him back to an exam room, and ten minutes later, Dr. Hillman came in, brought up the latest images they'd taken and pointed out his concerns.

"The crack appears to be mending," Dr. Hillman said, as he studied the new X-ray on the screen. "So that doesn't concern me. But you've got a torn patellar tendon, which is causing all the pain. You're going to need to take it easy, and once the swelling goes down, I'm going to order some physical therapy."

"I'll admit that I pushed myself too hard for a while, but now that I'm back home, I've made a point of taking it easy."

"Good." Dr. Hillman showed him the ultrasound scan. "I'm afraid both you and that bull have done a real number on that tendon. Bones usually heal faster than tissue. But the problem with this particular tear is that it could turn into patellar tendinitis if you're not careful, and that can have painful, crippling and lifelong consequences if not allowed to heal properly."

Matt braced himself for the answer to his biggest question. "But it will heal. Right? Completely?"

"With time." Dr. Hillman turned away from his computer screen to face Matt and crossed his arms. "I know how important it is for you to get back to competing, so let's take another look at your knee in three to four weeks."

That long? *After* the Rocking Chair Rodeo took place? Matt blew out a ragged sigh. "So, no riding until then?"

"I wouldn't recommend it—unless you're willing to risk a far more serious consequence that could keep you from any rodeo competition for the rest of your life, not to mention many day-to-day activities." The doctor placed his hand on Matt's shoulder and gave it a gentle squeeze. "Athletes tend to recover sooner than those who aren't as healthy and strong, but sometimes they don't take the time for their bodies to recover and push themselves too hard. And then all bets are off."

Again, Matt blew out a sigh.

"Hey," Dr. Hillman said, "no one gets this better than I do. I was a long distance runner in college, so I know what I'm talking about. You need to take off that mask and cape and give your body the time it needs."

"Okay. Got it."

"I'm also going to prescribe a brace that will help to stabilize your knee, as well as a pain medication."

"I…uh…already have some medication and a brace," Matt admitted. "I have a cane, too, but I…"

A wry grin slid across the doctor's face. "A real tough guy, huh? Well, the choice is yours, but I'd put it back on and wear it if I were you."

Matt nodded. "Okay. Thanks, Doc."

As soon as the doctor left the exam room, Matt limped to the front office, settled the bill and paid his deductible.

You'd think he'd have been happy to finally have his questions answered, especially by someone he'd come to trust, but those answers weren't the ones he'd hoped for.

Once he got back in the truck, he checked his cell and saw that Clay had called while his phone had been on silent. But Matt wouldn't return the call yet. He was still trying to wrap his mind around the news the doctor had given him, which would require an attitude adjustment. And that wasn't going to be easy for a guy who cherished his mask and cape.

In the meantime, he headed home. He couldn't stay away from the Double G forever.

Since it was nearing the dinner hour, he called the house to ask about the mealtime plans. If Miranda wasn't in the kitchen cooking and George had yet to open any cans of whatever simple fare he'd stored in the pantry, Matt would be happy to pick up something at one of the local restaurants or a drive-through and take it home.

The phone rang several times before George answered by saying, "I don't know who this is, but I hope you have a darn good reason for dragging me away from watching *Lonesome Dove*."

Matt laughed. If anyone had been counting, his uncle had probably watched that Western miniseries on television twenty-three times or more.

"I don't want to keep you from your favorite evening entertainment," Matt said. "I just need to know if you guys want me to bring something home for dinner. Or does Miranda plan to cook tonight?"

"She probably won't be home in time to eat, so get whatever you'd like. I've been munching on tortilla chips and guacamole, so I'm not too hungry."

"Where is she?"

"Miranda? She and Emily have spent the last couple of days at the county fairgrounds with the other kids and their lambs."

No wonder it had been so easy for him to avoid her. "When's the auction?"

"Tomorrow. At one o'clock, I think. Are you going?"

"Of course." What kind of dad skipped out on an event that was important to his daughter? Actually, Matt knew exactly what kind of father would do that. And years ago, he'd sworn not to follow in those lousy footsteps.

"I wouldn't miss it for the world," he added.

"I'm a little surprised, though."

At that, Matt gripped the steering wheel a little tighter. "About what?"

"Emily agreeing to auction off her lamb. She loves Bob. And the animal loves her, too. She doesn't even need a halter or a lead. It follows her wherever she goes."

"You're probably right," Matt said. "I have a feeling it's going to be hard for her to let him go. Especially knowing he'll end up as lamb stew on someone's dinner table."

"Yeah. That's what I'm thinking. But when I mentioned the auction, she seemed excited and told me that some of the other kids got over a thousand dollars for their lambs last year."

Damn. With a business sense like that, Emily might have more Contreras blood than Matt had realized. He supposed that wasn't a bad thing to have, as long as she didn't let it go to her head.

And Matt would have to make sure that it didn't.

"About dinner," Matt said. "I'll pick up a couple of

cheeseburgers. You're not hungry now, but you might be later tonight."

"That sounds good to me. And while you're at it, pick up an order of fries and a chocolate milkshake for me, too."

So much for filling up on chips and guacamole. Matt let out a little chuckle and slowly shook his head. "You got it. But what about Miranda?"

"What about her?" His uncle's jovial tone suggested that the man who didn't like to pry was doing just that.

Curiosity was probably eating him up, especially after he caught Matt and Miranda kissing on Monday night. But even if Matt wanted to open up to his uncle, he still didn't have a clue what he ought to do about it—if anything. So he didn't bite and skirted the issue instead.

"Will Miranda be home later tonight?" he asked. "If so, I can get something for her and Emily, too."

"I'm not sure when she'll be in, but it might be a good idea to get something for them, just to be safe. And you probably know this, but I'll mention it anyway. She prefers chicken over beef."

Matt had noticed that.

"By the way," George said, "I have a question for you. And I want to know the truth."

The direct approach, huh? Matt rolled his eyes. He hadn't just been avoiding Miranda so he didn't have to talk about that blasted kiss, he'd been avoiding George, too. And for the same reason.

He braced himself for the inevitable and said, "Fire away."

"How'd your visit with the doctor go? What did he have to say?"

That wasn't the question Matt had expected to hear. "How'd you know I saw a doctor?"

"Clay called a few minutes ago. He tried to reach you on your cell, but you didn't answer. So he thought you might be home."

Matt hadn't planned to tell anyone that he'd been concerned about his recovery and that he was getting a second opinion. Other than Clay, of course. But it was too late to backpedal now.

"I'll be okay." Eventually. And *hopefully*. "It's just going to take a little more time." And sadly, way more than he'd expected.

"At least you'll be okay in the long run," George said.

"Yeah, but not in time to compete at the Rocking Chair Rodeo. And I hate letting everyone down."

"So what are you going to do?"

"It's still two weeks away, so I'll have to take it day by day."

And that's just the same plan he'd make for dealing with Miranda.

Miranda got home late from the fairgrounds, tired and ready to call it a day. But when she spotted Matt's truck parked near the barn, her breath caught and a surge of adrenaline revived her. She hadn't known when he'd return from his business trip, but she'd hoped he would be home in time for the auction. That is, if he wanted to attend. Emily would be disappointed if he didn't.

She glanced in the rearview mirror at her daughter, who'd fallen asleep on the drive home. Had Miranda not been pregnant, she might have tried to carry Emily inside and put her to bed. As it was, she opted to wake the sleepy child and guide her to the back door.

The house was dark, so she assumed that both George and Matt had turned in for the night, which was just as well. She wasn't up for a chat.

After putting Emily to bed, tucking her in and kissing her brow, Miranda returned to the kitchen for a cookie and a glass of milk, a bedtime snack she hoped would tide her over until breakfast.

When she opened the fridge, she spotted two boxed meals on the center shelf, which she suspected had come from Caroline's Diner. She assumed Matt had brought dinner home for them, which had been a nice gesture. But one she refused to read into. They'd shared an amazing kiss last Monday, but they'd never talked about it. And to be honest, she was afraid to think about it too long. Nor was she crazy enough to ask Matt how he felt about it.

So once she'd eaten an Oreo and downed her milk, she made her way to her bedroom and climbed into bed, too tired to think.

Morning rolled around before she knew it, and by the time she'd showered, dressed and headed to the kitchen, everyone else had beat her there. George stood at the stove flipping pancakes, while Emily was perched on the counter beside him, watching his every move.

But it was Matt who caught Miranda's eye and demanded her full attention.

He sat leisurely at the table, a mug of black coffee in his hand. He'd shaved, nicking his chin in the process, but that didn't mar him in the least. His hair, still damp from the shower, was stylishly mussed. When their gazes met, her heart took a tumble. Memories of that heated kiss she'd tried to forget came flooding back, threatening to carry her away.

Darn it. If Matt stuck around the Double G much longer, she'd have to find another place to live. And quickly. She wasn't going to hold up very well if she had to face him each morning.

"I hope you're hungry," George said, a raised spatula in hand. "It's going to be a long day for all of us, and a good one. So I whipped up some of my famous hotcakes. You had them once before, Miranda, and you said you liked them. And I got a bottle of that blueberry syrup, too."

Yes, of course.

Blueberry pancakes.

Breakfast.

She turned away from Matt, tamping down the thoughts she shouldn't have, the dreams she had no business resurrecting and blessed his uncle with an appreciative smile. "Yes, you make the best pancakes in the world. But I'd better only have one. I'm a little too excited to eat."

Actually, she was more nervous than excited. And not just about Matt and the kiss they'd shared.

She studied her bright-eyed daughter, who didn't

seem the least bit concerned about that auction, which seemed a little odd for an animal lover who'd bonded with Bob the day they'd brought him to the ranch.

"How 'bout you?" George asked Matt. "That coffee's gonna burn a hole in your gizzard if you don't put something else in your belly."

"You're not much of a cook," Matt said, "but your hotcakes are the best I've ever eaten. I doubt Caroline could make better. So yes, Uncle George. I'll take a short stack."

While Emily chattered away, Miranda put a cup of water in the microwave and set the timer for two minutes. After the beep sounded, she removed it and brewed a single serving of herbal tea.

"I can't wait to go to the fair," Emily said. "I bet me and Bob win a blue ribbon."

"What time are we supposed to get there?" Matt asked.

"I forget. I'll have to check." Emily jumped down from the counter and made her way to the fridge where they'd posted the flyer with a magnet.

Apparently, Matt planned to go with them, which was both personally unsettling and a maternal relief. But she shook off her uneasiness, glad to know his presence would make Emily happy. For that reason, she caught his eye and smiled gratefully.

Like usual, when she tried to silently show her appreciation, he answered with a half-shrug, as if it were no big deal. But this was a special day for their daughter, and his being there to cheer her on was huge.

"The fair opens at nine o'clock," Emily said. "And

after I check on Bob and make sure he's okay, we can walk around and look at stuff."

"That'll give us time to go on a few rides, too. I'm looking forward to riding the roller coaster with you." Matt winked at the little girl. "That is, if you're not afraid."

"Hey!" Emily slapped her hands on her hips. "I'm not scared to ride it. I saw it yesterday and it's super big. But it'll be fun." Emily turned to Miranda. "Will you go with us, Mom?"

And ignore the signs that warned pregnant women not to get on any wild rides?

"Not today." She placed her hand on her belly and caressed her growing baby bump. "I'll have more fun watching you."

Besides, now that Matt had reentered her life, she'd already boarded an emotional roller coaster that was taking her through more ups and downs than she liked.

Chapter Nine

Matt and Miranda, along with George and Emily, drove to the county fairgrounds right after breakfast. They parked in the main lot, which was filling fast, and headed to the barns to visit Bob.

Emily slipped into his pen, dropped to her knees and gave the lamb a hug. Then she kissed his wooly head. "You look so handsome with your new haircut, Bob. Everyone is going to see that you're the best lamb here."

George placed a curved hand to his mouth and mumbled something to Matt. Miranda strained to hear what he was saying, only to pick up a few words and phrases.

"I don't know 'bout this..."

"Bob? Should be Shish ka-Bob."

"You sure she knows...?"

Miranda caught enough to know what he meant. A similar thought had crossed her mind more than once. Emily didn't seem to mind that Bob was going on the auction block, which was surprising because she was so fond of him. But apparently she was okay with it because she'd already begun to list the things she wanted to buy with her money. And she'd even mentioned her plan to donate a hundred dollars to Rick's animal rescue operation.

After letting herself out of Bob's pen, Emily said, "We have to be back by twelve-thirty. But we can go on the rides until then."

"Then what are we waiting for?" Matt asked. "Let's check out that roller coaster and see if it's as big as you said it was."

They exited the barn, then walked through the exhibit hall and out to the actual fairgrounds. Excitement filled the air, along with the tantalizing smell of candied apples, peanuts and cotton candy.

It was still early in the day, but people were already in line to purchase deep-fried Twinkies and a variety of almost every other packaged pastry imaginable.

Matt stopped by the ticket booth and pulled out his wallet to purchase a package of tickets. He'd worn a knee brace today. Miranda first thought his leg must be bothering him, but then she realized he'd probably come prepared to do a lot of walking.

In the distance, children laughed and shrieked with glee, while a baby needing a nap or some cuddling began to fuss.

"There it is!" Emily pointed to the roller coaster. "See? I told you it was super big."

Matt reached for her hand. "Then let's go."

As the rodeo champ limped along with the excited child, Miranda couldn't help admiring him—and not just his awesome physical appearance. He wasn't letting a bad knee stop him from spending the day with his daughter and making sure she was having fun.

By the time Miranda and George caught up with them, Matt and Emily had settled into one of the cars, just as a ride attendant lowered the lap bar and locked it in place.

As their train of cars rolled off in a wheel-churning, metal-creaking rush, a thrill shot through Miranda, and she felt as if she were riding along with them, even though she remained on the sidelines with George.

By the time Matt and Emily reached the first peak on the track and began their descent, they raised their hands in the air. Matt, who must have taught Emily the fine art of roller coaster riding, laughed. And Emily squealed in both fear and delight.

Miranda placed her hand on her baby bump and reminded herself not to lose her head and let her emotions run away with her. No matter how she'd felt about Matt in the past, the young cowboy she'd once loved was long gone. And even if his lovemaking had been honed and was far better than she remembered, the kiss they'd shared the other night didn't mean a thing and would have to remain a sweet memory. She'd have to be content knowing that her happy daughter not only looked up to her father, but she adored him, too. And

Matt appeared to feel the same way about her. Only a fool would ask for any more than that.

When the roller coaster ride came to an end, Matt gave Emily a high five before climbing out of the car. As they approached Miranda and George, Matt's limp seemed a little more pronounced, but he wore a brighter smile.

Again, Miranda had to remind herself that she'd be foolish to dream of having any more than she already had—a happy child, a renewed friendship with the man she'd once loved, a man who was proving to be a good father.

But when Matt's gazed locked on hers, and her heart spun out of control, she feared that she was more foolish than she'd ever thought possible.

For nearly two hours, Emily led Matt from one carnival ride to another, while George and Miranda tagged along behind them, and the exuberant child didn't slow down until Matt insisted that it was time to take a break and get something to eat.

"That's a good idea." Miranda wanted to get off her feet, too. She should have worn different shoes because the new flats she'd chosen had rubbed her right heel raw. She'd have to look to be sure, but she suspected she'd find a blister.

"I'll tell ya what." George reached into his back pocket and pulled out his beat-up wallet. "If you'll take a seat at this table, I'll spring for lunch. Any one up for chili dogs? They can be a little messy, but they sure are good."

"I don't like chilies or cheese," Emily said. "I only want ketchup on mine."

Miranda and Matt both opted for regular hot dogs.

"All right-y," George said. "I'll have 'em pack up those dogs and all the fixin's, then I'll bring them back to you."

"Thanks. That'd be great." Matt took a seat, stretched out his bad leg and used his fingers to stroke his knee through the metal hinges on his brace.

"After we eat a good lunch, can we have cotton candy for dessert?" Emily asked.

Matt glanced at his cell phone. "We'd better wait to have dessert until after the auction. It's almost noon, and we'll need to head back to the barn pretty soon."

Forty-five minutes later, after they left Emily at the barn, they headed to the grandstand and took their seats, with Miranda in the middle.

"You've been a real trouper today," Miranda told Matt. "How are you holding up?"

"I'm okay." He glanced at her lap, where her hands had clasped around her belly, then looked up and caught her gaze. "How about you?"

Rather than respond to the quiet implication that pregnancy might be slowing her down, she skated over it by removing her right shoe and wiggling her toes. "Other than a blister on my heel, I'm holding up just fine." She nodded at his bad leg. "I'm more concerned about you. I hope you haven't set yourself back."

"You and me both. But I didn't have the heart to disappoint Emily when she was having so much fun."

"I know what you mean. Her enthusiasm can be a

little annoying sometimes, but I actually admire it."
Miranda admired Matt, too. He was turning out to be
a good father, one Emily could look up to. A man she
could be proud of.

Matt cocked his head slightly and eyed her face.

"What's the matter?" she asked.

He reached out and placed his index finger at the
side of her mouth, stroking her skin and sparking a
heated tingle that rushed down her throat and to her
chest.

Her breath caught. She would have asked what he
was doing, but she was so stunned by his touch that
she couldn't form a single word.

"You've got a little mustard there," he said. "But
I got it."

She opened her mouth to thank him for caring
enough to save her the embarrassment of walking
around the fairgrounds with the remnant of her lunch
on her face. But what if she stuttered and stammered?
What if he realized his touch still had a blood-stirring
effect on her?

She cleared her throat, shaking one single word free.
"Thanks."

Matt merely nodded, then pointed to the arena and
the parade of children and their lambs now entering.

George was the first to spot Emily and Bob. "Will
you look at that? She's doing great. She's leaving plenty
of room between Bob and the other lambs. And she's
making sure his legs are set and that his head is up
and alert."

"And she's keeping her eyes on the judge," Miranda added. "Just like she's supposed to."

"She's a born showman," Matt said.

Miranda pulled out her cell phone and began snapping pictures.

"Looks like you're having a proud mama moment," George said.

Miranda laughed. "You've got that right."

They craned their necks as they watched Emily show her lamb, going through the drills she'd practiced daily since Bob's arrival on the Double G.

After the judge handed Emily a red ribbon, she dropped to her knees in front of her lamb, cupped his face with her hands and pressed a kiss on his snout. Then she gave him a hug.

"Looks like she's having a proud mama moment, too," Matt said.

"Maybe so." George sat back in his seat and gripped the armrests. "But I don't have a good feeling about this."

"Neither do I," Miranda said. "But so far, she seems to be okay with it. I guess we'll have to wait and see how she does after the auction."

They didn't have to wait long. Ten minutes later, Bob was on the block. As the bids increased, Emily appeared delighted. And when he sold for nearly fifteen-hundred dollars, she lifted her hands to clap, then slapped them back at her sides as if remembering to curb her enthusiasm and to be a good sport.

"Her attitude blows me away," Matt said. "That girl definitely has ranching in her blood."

After the young handlers turned over their lambs to the ring steward, Emily scanned the grandstand until she spotted where her family sat. Then she hurried to-ward the fence.

Even though she lowered her voice, she couldn't hide her excitement. "Bob did it," she whispered. "He won a lot of money. Now I can buy another lamb. And I can give some money to Dr. Rick for his pet rescue, too."

Miranda looked at Matt, who shrugged as if he didn't know what to say.

When Emily started to turn back toward the ring, where the stewards were herding the lambs through a gate, she stopped in her tracks and glanced over her shoulder at Miranda, Matt and George. "Hey! Where are they taking Bob and those other lambs?"

"The man who just bought them is..." Miranda hated to remind her that they'd be taken to a slaugh-terhouse—eventually. "He's taking the lambs that he purchased."

"*What*?" Her eyes widened, and her jaw dropped. "He *bought* Bob?"

"Yes, in the auction."

"But Bob is *my* lamb. I want to take him *home*."

"I'm afraid you can't do that. I thought that you under-stood what was going to happen at the auction. Weren't you listening when they explained...?" Miranda paused, unable to complete the sentence, especially when it was now obvious the child hadn't paid attention.

"When you agreed to auction Bob, it meant you agreed to sell him. It meant that he'd..." Matt paused.

Miranda picked up where he left off, hoping to soften the blow. "That he'd have to go to someone else's ranch."

Emily's lip quivered, and tears welled in her eyes. "But I thought *auctioned* meant that they were going to give me money as a prize for taking such good care of him and for teaching him to obey and be good. What's that man going to do with him? Keep him? Put him in a pen with a bunch of other sheep he doesn't even know?"

Miranda didn't have the heart to reveal Bob's fate, and she looked at Matt, hoping he'd find the words once more.

But Matt only gazed at their daughter, who was now sobbing hard enough for her tears to fill a water trough. And if the sympathy Miranda read in his expression was a clue, it appeared that he might fall apart, too.

"I'll be right back," he said, as he got to his feet.

"Where are you going?" Miranda asked.

"To make a deal with the guy who bought her lamb. I might have to offer him more money than he spent, but I'm not going to turn my back on family. And apparently, Bob is now part of mine."

Miranda's heart soared, and her plan to keep Matt at an emotionally safe distance failed. Because she'd just fallen hopelessly in love with him all over again.

That evening, after driving everyone home and putting Emily's beloved pet back in his pen, Matt suggested they go to Mario's Pizzeria to celebrate Bob's return to the fold.

"That sounds good to me," Miranda said. "This has been the kind of day I'd love to celebrate."

Love? She cringed inwardly at the slip up. She hadn't meant to use the *L* word when talking to Matt, even though she'd meant dealing with her child's meltdown and walking all over the fairground until she ended up with a good-sized blister on one heel and a small one on the other.

George slowly shook his balding head. "You guys go on ahead without me. Those two chili-cheese dogs I wolfed down at the fair gave me indigestion."

"We can bring something home for you," Matt said. "You might feel better later and want to eat then."

"Don't bother." George tapped his fist against his upper chest a couple of times. "The last thing I want to eat tonight is something loaded down with pepperoni, sausage and spicy Italian tomato sauce."

"We could order a plain cheese pizza for you and ask them to hold the sauce," Miranda said.

George blew out a humph. "What kind of Texas rancher do you think I am? I wouldn't eat a tasteless, wimpy pizza like that on a bet." Then he topped off the snarky comment with a wink.

Miranda felt a little uneasy about leaving him home alone, although she wasn't sure why. Those two chili-cheese dogs had been covered with onions and topped with jalapeños. So it didn't surprise her that he was suffering indigestion now. Still…

"I realize you never have liked doctors," Miranda said, "but I also know you've seen one recently. Maybe you should give him or her a call and mention that indigestion. I also noticed that you've gotten a little out of breath lately."

George waved her off. "Me and the doc have it all under control. It's nothing a little pill or two won't fix. So you don't need to worry about me."

"All right," she said. "I'm glad you're taking care of yourself."

"I appreciate your concern," he said, "but I'll be right as rain after I take a couple of antacids."

He was probably right, so they left him home and went to the pizzeria without him.

Miranda had planned to check on him later that night, after they returned from Mario's, but by the time they'd entered the back door, the house was quiet and the lights had been dimmed. Clearly, he'd already turned in for the night.

But why wouldn't he? They'd all had a long, exciting day. Even Emily's shoulders had begun to droop, so Miranda told her it was time for bed.

"Aw, man." Emily rolled her eyes, but the effort lacked her usual dramatic flair. "Okay, but can I skip my bath tonight?"

"Absolutely not. And don't forget to brush your teeth."

Apparently, Emily couldn't come up with a reasonable argument because she turned on her heel and did as she was told.

"Matt," Miranda said, "if you're up for some decaf, I'll brew a small pot for you and then steep a cup of tea for me."

"Sounds good."

She would have suggested that they take their drinks out to the front porch, but she didn't want him to think she was trying to set up a repeat of Monday night. If they were to go outdoors, it would have to be his idea. And if that were the case, she'd jump at the chance, even though no good would come of it.

"I'd offer to help you in the kitchen," Matt said, "but my knee is killing me. I'd better plop my butt on the sofa and give it a rest."

She offered him a smile. "If I hadn't kicked off my shoes when we got home from the fair and traded them for a pair of flip-flops, I'd pass on the tea and plop down next to you."

Ten minutes later, Miranda placed a white coffee mug and her favorite teacup, both filled with their respective steaming hot brews, onto a wicker tray and carried it into the living room. After setting it on the coffee table, she took a seat on the sofa, next to the armrest, which put a wise and healthy space between them.

Rather than reach for his coffee, Matt stretched out his leg and removed the brace.

"How's your knee feeling?" she asked.

"A little achy today. But overall, it's about the same."

"No worse?" She nodded at the brace. "You weren't wearing that before."

"Actually, I was, but I took it off before I drove home to the Double G. Apparently—" he paused for a couple of beats "—I shouldn't have done that. I might have screwed it up for good. And if that's the case, I'll have to give up the rodeo, which I don't want to do."

He'd have to give up the fame, too, she supposed. But that really wasn't any of her business.

"You have no idea how much I appreciate all you did today," she said.

"It was no big deal."

"Oh, but it was. Emily couldn't be happier, and I... Well, I'm just glad the two of you are bonding."

"Me, too. But..."

She waited for him to continue, to explain, but it became a long wait. She lifted the delicate china teacup and saucer from the tray and sat back on the sofa.

"I'm not sure if you remember," Matt said, "but my dad and I didn't have a good relationship. We still don't. So when it comes to parenthood, I'm in uncharted territory."

"I do remember, and I'm sorry things never got any better between you. But just so you know, I think you were a perfect dad today."

Matt seemed to mull that over, then smiled. "You mean by offering to whip out my checkbook to save the day? What else could I do? You saw how heartbroken she was when she thought she'd lost her lamb. Besides, the fair adjusted the buyer's bill, and I didn't have to actually pay anything."

"I realize that, but you went to bat for Emily when you convinced the buyer to let us take Bob home. And you also trekked all over the fairgrounds with a bad knee. The way I see it, after today, you've already proven to Emily that you're the best daddy ever."

"Thanks. I appreciate that. But there'll probably be other days when things don't turn out so well."

"True. I've had days like that."

Matt lifted his mug, took a drink and said, "Rumor has it that Emily wants to get another lamb. A *girl one* so they can have a baby."

Miranda laughed and rolled her eyes. "The last thing she needs is another animal. And even if I would've let her buy a second lamb with the auction money— which I wouldn't have done—she can't afford it now. Besides, we can't stay at the Double G forever, and depending upon where we end up, she might not be able to take her animals with her. At least, not all of them."

"What are your plans?" he asked.

"I'm going to put my condo in San Antonio on the market and relocate, hopefully to a place with enough property for Emily's menagerie."

"Does that mean you'd consider relocating here?"

"That's what I'm thinking. Emily and I both like living in Brighton Valley, and she's making friends at school and in the 4-H Club. Hopefully, my dad will let me work remotely. Because if I do find a place and move here, I can't very well commute to San Antonio on a regular basis."

And if she couldn't work for Contreras Farms, she'd need to find another way to support herself and her growing family.

She glanced down at her lap, which seemed to be disappearing more and more each week. She'd also have to find a competent nanny.

When she looked up again, she caught Matt gazing at her.

"So you still haven't told your father?" he asked.

"I was going to, but then I got busy with all the county fair prep and 4-H activities, so I put it off for another week. But I can't wait much longer."

Matt didn't respond. He didn't even make a snide remark about her dad, which he'd been doing ever since he arrived at his uncle's ranch. So she took this as a good sign that they seemed to be working through the past.

"What about *your* dad?" she asked. "Have you talked to him?"

"About Emily? No, not yet. And I really don't want to. He'd probably ask to meet her, and I don't want him to disappoint her the way he disappointed me."

Miranda wouldn't want to see that happen, either. But maybe the man would turn out to be a better grandfather than a father.

"It sounds to me like you still keep in touch with him," she said.

"I guess you could say that. He calls me every few weeks, although I never have much to say to him. He wasn't much of a father, but then again, he didn't think I was much of a son."

She'd hoped that, over the past nine years, Matt and his father would've buried the hatchet, but apparently they hadn't. From what little the old Matt had told her in the past, his father had really hurt him. And it didn't look like the new Matt had gotten over it.

Matt took another drink of coffee, then he turned toward her. "Why have you waited so long to tell your dad about the baby? I'd think you'd want to get it over with."

She drew in a deep breath, held it for a beat, then let it out slowly. "If I had my way, I'd wait to tell my dad until the baby takes his first step."

Matt's brow furrowed as he pondered her response.

She probably should explain. "When he finds out, he'll pressure me to return to San Antonio, which I'll have to do anyway when I sell the condo and line up the movers. But once I'm back in the city, Gavin is bound to find out I'm pregnant. And I'd rather that didn't happen until it's not as easy for him to do the math and realize the baby is his."

Matt arched a brow. "I thought you said you weren't afraid of Gavin."

"I'm not afraid for myself. It's just that he might petition the court for visitation, and I know the baby wouldn't be safe with him. So I've been dragging my feet to protect both kids, since I don't want him showing up at my house—even for holidays."

Matt pondered her words for a beat, then said, "If Gavin had any suspicions, you could tell him the baby's mine."

Chapter Ten

You could tell him the baby's mine.

Damn. Hearing himself blurt out a suggestion like that surprised Matt as much as it had clearly taken Miranda aback. Then again, maybe not.

She continued to gape at him, her eyes wide and unblinking, as if he'd shown up at a rodeo wearing only his hat and boots. The fingers that held the delicate handle of that fancy pink teacup trembled until she lifted her free hand to steady it. But even supporting it with two hands didn't seem to help much.

Matt reached for the teacup before she dropped it to the floor, took it from her and placed it on the saucer that rested on the coffee table.

At that, Miranda blinked, and her stunned expression shifted into one that appeared more perplexed.

"Are you serious?" she asked.

He wasn't sure. He hadn't planned to offer her any advice, but for some stupid reason, the words had rolled off his tongue the second that wild solution had come to mind.

But what was he worried about? It wasn't as if he'd offered to pay her child support on an eighteen-year plan—and for a kid who wasn't his.

So he shrugged off his reservations and gave her the best explanation he had. "You're not the only one who doesn't want that guy showing up at your house."

A deep crease in the center of her brow suggested that she might be pondering his crazy idea and considering any other options she might have.

He doubted that she could come up with anything else that would keep Gavin out of her life.

Maybe she was worried about the possible repercussions they could face if they did lie about the baby's paternity. And there were sure to be some.

Her father's temper came to mind. The man had an image to protect, and he would have a conniption fit if he thought Matt had fathered another one of Miranda's kids, both of who were illegitimate.

Not that Matt got any pleasure from Miranda's current situation—neither this pregnancy nor the one he'd been responsible for. Besides, he would have married her in a heartbeat if she would have told him about Emily.

As he thought about her father's reaction to the news of Matt being the father of her second child, a smile began to form, and he almost chuckled.

Apparently, there was still a rebellious spirit inside of him, waiting on the sidelines, flexing its muscles and ready to jump into the fray, just to set off Miranda's old man.

"You know," Miranda said, "if you're actually serious, that idea just might work. How do you see this all playing out?"

Other than pissing off her dad? Matt really hadn't thought it through. So he asked, "What's the worst thing that could happen?"

"Well, at first, my father would probably want to punch your lights out."

From what Matt had heard, Carlos Contreras wasn't a man most people wanted to cross. But he'd been in his forties when Miranda was born, so he must be pushing seventy now. And since he'd quit working in the fields years ago, he'd probably gotten soft and would think twice about raising his fists.

"Things won't get physical," Matt said. "That is, unless your dad gets violent. But either way, I'm not afraid of him. So what else could happen?"

"I suppose Gavin could ask for a DNA test."

"He might. But then he'd probably rather not have to pay you any child support."

"You're probably right."

"And if he doesn't ask for proof of paternity, you wouldn't get the money."

"I don't need it."

She hadn't needed child support from Matt, either, which clamped a vise on his ego and tightened it. But he shook it off. There was no need to poke at the past.

"Just to make it clear," he said, "I'd walk away before risking a loud or physical altercation with your father. And I suspect Gavin won't ask for a DNA test. If he did, he'd have to deal with charges that he hit Emily. That might give him reason to reconsider."

She cocked her head slightly and studied him carefully, most likely trying to read into his offer and his take on all of it. But damn, when she looked at him like that, feelings rose up in his chest. Soft and tender ones that made him want to pull her into his arms and promise her the moon, tell her he'd do anything to make her happy and to keep her and the children safe.

"Listen," he said, tamping down the rising emotion that wouldn't do either one of them any good, "I just threw that idea out there to make sure you and the kids never have to deal with Gavin again."

"You want to protect the baby, too?" she asked, her voice soft, tender.

"Of course. It's not his fault that he has a crappy biological dad." Nor had it been Matt's fault that he'd been cursed with a lousy one, either.

"But what about the baby's birth date?" she asked. "I was engaged to Gavin until February, so he's going to know that he's the father."

"You can tell Gavin and other people that the baby came early. Or if it arrives weighing a whopping nine or ten pounds, we can say that you and I crossed paths at the end of last year. The old feelings we had for each other were hard to ignore, and we couldn't help ourselves. It just happened."

Miranda turned to face him, and as her gaze targeted his, a rush of desire swept over him. The explanation he'd just given her took on a life of its own, and he could see how a heated moment might occur when two old lovers met.

She didn't say anything, but she didn't have to. The emotion welling in her eyes told him all he needed to hear, all he needed to know.

Talk about old memories, sudden realizations and a burst of heat. He cupped her face, and her lips parted. As his fingers slipped along her jaw and around to the back of her neck, her glossy locks cascaded over his hand. Then he drew her mouth to his.

He hadn't planned to kiss her. If he had, he would've started out softly, tenderly, making the moment last. But the second their lips touched, his brain checked out completely and thoughts like *slow* and *easy* went right out the window.

Apparently, Miranda didn't mind things taking off like a blast from the past. She leaned into him, her hands re-exploring his body. Her lips parted, allowing his tongue to sweep into her mouth to mate with hers, dipping and twisting and tasting until he thought he'd explode.

But kissing Miranda senseless was one thing.

Taking her to bed was another.

Mustering every bit of strength and self-control he had, Matt ended the earthshaking kiss, but he didn't pull away. He continued to hold her close, savoring the chance to have her in his arms again, the faint scent of her floral shampoo, the warmth of her breath against his skin.

"See what I mean?" He rested his forehead against hers, and a slow smile curved his mouth. "Things like this happen when old lovers run into each other."

She didn't agree, but she didn't let go of him, either.

"Do you see how things could easily get out of control?"

At that, she drew back, and her passion-glazed eyes met his. "We shouldn't let that happen."

"We shouldn't?"

Her lips parted, as if she had a ready answer, but she didn't say another word.

Hell, she probably didn't dare to, because there was no way she'd convince him that a few bedroom thoughts hadn't crossed her mind as well. And there lay the problem.

Things were heading in a sexual direction, and as much as he'd taken the lead and enjoyed what they'd just done, he wasn't sure whether he should thank his lucky stars for that amazing kiss or run for the hills while he still had the chance.

The next day, after they'd eaten turkey sandwiches and apple slices for lunch, Matt continued to hang out at the kitchen table, hoping to find time to talk to Miranda alone. He had an idea he wanted to share with her, and this one wasn't as wild and crazy as the one he'd suggested last night.

Since she'd just asked Emily to help her clear the table, the chat he had planned to have with her would have to wait.

George, who'd left the table earlier, returned to the

kitchen with his hair damp and combed and wearing a different shirt than the one he'd had on before.

"Miranda," he said, "I've got a few errands to run in town. Would it be okay if I took the little munchkin with me?"

Emily cocked her head, furrowed her brow and looked at Matt. "What's a munchkin?"

"The munchkins are characters in *The Wizard of Oz*," he said. "Have you seen the movie?"

She shook her head no.

"That's too bad," he said, "It's a classic. I guess we'll have to schedule a movie night."

"That's a good idea," Miranda added. "We can make popcorn and root beer floats."

"That sounds fun." Emily leaned toward Matt, cupped a hand at the side of her mouth and lowered her voice. "But why did he call me that?"

"It's not always easy to know what your uncle is thinking." Matt winked at George.

"I like to keep some things to myself, but I'll tell you what I've got on my mind today." George lobbed a smile at Emily. "A big bowl of frozen yogurt. And maybe even a visit to the feed store to check out what kind of critters they've got on special today. If your mom says it's okay, I'd be happy to take you with me."

Emily clapped her hands and turned to Miranda. "Can I, Mommy? Please."

"Yes," Miranda said. "But don't bring home any animals. You have more than enough pets already."

George chuckled on the way out, while Emily trotted along behind him.

After the door closed, Matt studied Miranda, who'd turned back around to wipe down the kitchen counter. She wore a yellow sundress today, reminding him of the roses he'd once given her back in the day.

But it was the future he wanted to broach. So he opened by saying, "I've been thinking about something."

She turned around, her brow raised in apprehension. "About what?"

"About job opportunities. If your dad won't let you work remotely, I have an idea that might interest you."

The hesitation in her expression lightened. "What is it?"

"Have you heard of Kidville?"

"Yes, it's a local group home for abused and neglected kids. The Rocking Chair Rodeo is going to give it some of their proceeds."

"That's right. Jim Hoffman, one of the directors, is looking for someone, preferably a CPA, to handle the books. His wife, Donna, was doing it, but they're expanding Kidville, and she doesn't have the time. I'm not sure what they can afford to pay—or even if you'd be interested. But they're local."

"Thanks. If I end up needing to find another position, I'll definitely give them a call." She leaned against the kitchen counter. "I also had an idea of my own."

"Oh, yeah?" Matt asked. "What's that?"

"I have some money set aside for investments, and I thought about buying that pharmacy in town. I think the old-style soda fountain could really be a money-maker—if run properly. And if it also sold gifts and trinkets that would appeal to the tourists... Well, I think sales would increase."

"I like that idea." He also liked knowing that she was seriously planning to relocate to Brighton Valley. If she and Emily lived closer to the ranch, he'd be able to see them—and the baby, too—more often. Or at least every time he came home.

More importantly, though, she'd finally be pulling away from her father, which she'd needed to do for a long time.

"I'll have to talk it over with my dad first," she said. "A lot depends on whether I can work remotely for Contreras Farms. Either way, I'm moving to Brighton Valley."

"It'll be nice to have you living in town," he said.

She folded her arms across her chest, resting them on the top of her baby bump, and studied him for a couple of beats. "Okay, this is crazy."

"What is?"

"We've either ignored those two kisses or skated over them long enough."

She was right, although he'd still rather avoid having the conversation. He slowly got to his feet. He'd forgotten to wear the brace today, and that blasted tendon in his knee was already complaining. Maybe he ought to walk it off. Or else go back to his room and put the brace back on.

"Last night you implied that you were only kissing me to make a point," she said. "But I think there was a lot more to it than that."

As the accusation sunk in, so did the truth of it.

"You're right," he said.

"So what should we do about it?"

He shrugged. "Take it day by day, I guess."

"That makes sense."

"I won't deny that the chemistry is still there," he admitted. "But we probably shouldn't rush into anything sexual, even though that's a tempting idea."

"I agree."

"But that doesn't mean we can't do family stuff. I can always use more practice."

She smiled and leaned against the kitchen counter. "That day at the fair was awesome."

"And now we have a movie night to look forward to." Matt took a few steps, trying to shake the ache he'd gotten from sitting so long.

"I have a question for you," Miranda said.

"What's that?"

She placed a gentle, protective hand on her growing waistline, took a deep breath, bit down on her lower lip and lowered her gaze to the floor. After a couple of beats, she looked up again and blew out a sigh. "How will the baby fit into your idea of a family?"

Talk about cutting to the chase. But he really couldn't blame a mother for looking out for her child. In truth, she ought to be more concerned about how her father was going to fit into Matt's idea of a family.

"I don't see a problem." He crossed the kitchen, easing closer to Miranda, close enough to touch. He raised the palm of his hand toward her baby bump and asked, "Do you mind?"

She smiled, removed her hand and let her arm drop to her side. "No, not at all."

Matt had stroked the bellies of pregnant mares and heifers, but never an expectant mother. And as he felt a little bump move to the side of the womb—a foot, maybe?—his breath caught and his eyes opened in awe. "Wow. That's so cool."

And a miracle in the making.

He caught her gaze and smiled. "As far as I'm concerned, that little guy is my daughter's baby brother. And he'll always be a part of you. So I'll try my best to treat him as if he were my biological son."

She pressed her fingers against her lips, holding back either a sob or a response. Still, tears filled her eyes. "I'd hoped you would say that. But I was afraid that you might…"

"That I might not treat him fairly?" Matt reached out and, using his thumb, brushed a tear from her cheek. "I'll be damned if I'll ever show any favoritism to Emily over the baby. Or vice versa. And I'll do whatever it takes to make sure neither of them ever feels neglected or left out, the way I did when I was growing up."

"Does that mean you see a future for us? I mean as a family?"

"I guess that's what I'm saying."

The tears in Miranda's pretty caramel-colored eyes overflowed and spilled down her cheeks. This time, they flowed faster than he could wipe them away.

Matt had never felt comfortable around crying women, but this was different. Miranda was different.

"Don't worry," she said, sniffling. "I'm not sad or upset. These are happy tears."

He wrapped her in a warm embrace and drew her close. Happy or sad, he didn't like seeing her cry, so he stroked her back, offering whatever comfort he could. He wasn't sure how long they stood like that. A couple of minutes, maybe. He would have remained there for as long as she needed him to, but she was the first to pull away.

She looked up at him with a smile, and as their gazes met and locked in place, something passed between them, bonding them in an unexpected way.

He couldn't move, couldn't look away, couldn't think—until she ran the tip of her tongue along her lips, setting off a flurry of pheromones and hormones he hadn't experienced in a long, long time.

In spite of his resolve to take things one day at a time, his common sense and resolve dissipated in a rush of desire. And all he knew was that he didn't just want to kiss her again. He needed to.

As if reading his mind, she lifted her mouth to his, and they came together as if they'd never been apart.

Miranda was the last woman in the world Matt should be kissing, let alone making love with, but there wasn't much he could do about it now. Not when she was the only woman he'd ever really wanted.

So he took her by the hand. "Come here. I need to get off my feet."

When he led her away from the kitchen table and past the sofa in the living room, she asked, "Where are we going?"

He paused before reaching the hall. "Unless you have an objection, we're going to my bedroom."

Miranda continued to walk with Matt down the hall and into his room, her heart pounding, her blood racing. They stopped next to the bed, and he pulled her into his arms. She leaned into him, her baby bump pressing against him.

As their lips met, he swayed but quickly recovered.

"Are you sure you're okay?" she asked.

"My knee is messed up and hurts like hell most of the time. But don't worry. The other parts of me are in perfect working order. So I won't disappoint you."

At that, she laughed. "You never have."

"Good." He took a seat on the edge of the mattress, following through on the need to take the weight off his knee. "But what about you?"

"Me?"

He nodded at her growing belly. "Is it going to hurt anything if we make love?"

She smiled, appreciating his concern. "Between your knee and my baby bump, we might need to adjust our positions now and then."

"That's not going to be a problem." Matt drew her closer, bent his head and placed a kiss on her belly. When he looked up again, he blessed her with an old Matt grin. "I'll be careful with this little guy before and after he gets here."

Miranda didn't think she could ever love this man any more than she did right now. She brushed her lips against his forehead, and he drew her onto the bed, where he took her into his arms and placed his mouth on hers.

Their hands roamed each other's bodies, seeking, exploring, caressing. When Matt's hand worked its way to her breast, and his thumb skimmed across her nipple, she feared she would melt into a puddle on the bed if they didn't pull back the sheets and remove their clothes.

As a yearning emptiness settled deep in her core, she withdrew her lips from his. With a voice husky and laden with desire, she whispered, "I've really missed you, Matt. And I've missed this."

Matt had really missed her, too—more than he wanted to admit. He'd never ached for a woman this badly. And he doubted he ever would.

Unable and unwilling to prolong the foreplay any longer, he sat up in bed, unbuttoned his shirt, slipped it off and tossed it to the floor. Then he unbuckled his belt and undid the metal buttons on his jeans. As he peeled off his pants, he took care not to jar his knee.

When he'd removed his boxers, baring his body to her, she skimmed her nails across his chest, sending a heated shiver through his veins.

Her gaze never left his as she, too, sat up beside him. She lifted the hem of her yellow sundress, scooting and gathering the fabric until she could lift it over her head and toss it to the floor, next to his discarded clothes.

When she unhooked her bra, freeing her gorgeous breasts, much fuller now than before, he longed to take her in his arms. He wanted nothing more than to feel

the heat of her skin on his, to sink deep into her, showing her that he'd missed her, too, and letting her know
just how much.

Instead, he drank in the angelic sight he'd never
thought he'd see again. "You're beautiful."

A slow smile stretched across her lips. "You are,
too."

He didn't know about that, what with the few scars
he'd added since the last time they'd been together.

Unable to ignore the tempting view of her breasts
any longer, he took a nipple in his mouth, tonguing it,
loving it, then moving to the other until she gasped in
pleasure.

Taking mercy on them both, he laid her down and
rolled to his side, thanking his lucky stars that he had
her in his bed again, that he had the chance to savor
the sight of those luscious dark curls splayed on his
pillow, those expressive brown eyes glazed with pas-
sion as they watched his every move.

An easy grin spread across her face. "This is the
point where we used to need a condom."

He returned her smile. It would be nice to make
love without a barrier between them for a change. At
least that kind.

As he braced himself on an elbow, intending to
rise over her, she placed her hand on his shoulder and
pushed him back onto the mattress. "Under the circumstances, it might be better if I get on top."

"Good idea."

She moved slowly at first, taking care not to bump
his knee, but she soon settled onto his erection. His

body responded to hers, up and down, in and out, the world-shaking tempo setting his soul on fire.

He closed his eyes, savoring the magic they'd always created in this room and on this bed.

Their lives might be heading in a complicated direction, one they probably should reconsider, but not when their hormones were spinning out of control. As it always had in the past when they'd made love, time stood still, and the only thing that mattered was the two of them and the love they made.

When Miranda reached a peak, she cried out, arched her back and let it go. He shuddered as she climaxed, releasing with her in a sexual explosion that gave him a glimpse of the heavens and a glittery night sky filled with shooting stars.

Matt had no idea what the future would hold, but at least for this afternoon, she was his.

Chapter Eleven

As they lay in the afterglow of an amazing climax, Miranda nuzzled into Matt, savoring his familiar, mountain-fresh scent and the velvet hard feel of the man she'd never stopped loving.

"How's your knee?" she asked.

"It's all right, I guess." An unreadable expression crossed his face. "I mean, making love didn't make it any worse."

She rose up on her elbow and stroked his chest, her fingers tracing a curved scar she didn't remember him having, reminding her even more of the danger he faced each time he climbed on a bull. "But it's still bad. Isn't it?"

"Yeah." He pursed his lips and frowned. "What's worse, I'm not going to be able to compete in the Rocking Chair Rodeo."

"There'll be others," she said, telling him what she suspected he wanted to hear.

"I hope you're right, but the jury's still out on that."

Miranda tried to conjure more sympathy for him than she actually had. Even when they'd dated before, she'd known how he felt about the rodeo. He'd loved the roar of the crowd, the thrill of the ride—maybe even more than he'd claimed to love her.

It might be selfish on her part, but if truth be told, she didn't want him to return to the circuit for safety reasons. And there were a few emotional reasons, too. She didn't want him to return to the buckle bunnies who were known to fawn over their rodeo hero.

In so many other ways, Matt was her hero, too, and she didn't want to share him.

"I'm going to Houston tomorrow to meet with the Rocking Chair Rodeo promoters."

"How long will you be gone?" she asked.

"A couple of days."

Now that they were back together, she wasn't ready to lose him, even for that short of a time. "Do you have to go?"

"I made a commitment to bring in more sponsorships and to help the Rocking Chair Rodeo draw a big crowd. And I plan to follow through on it, even if I can't actually ride."

Matt might be medically grounded, and he appeared to be back in the saddle again, so to speak. But there was a lot more going on under on the surface.

If he couldn't compete again, his heart would be

broken. And if he did go back out on the circuit, hers would probably break instead.

In spite of how special, how amazing their lovemaking had been, that bittersweet truth buffed the shine off the afterglow.

Her chest ached, and tears pricked her eyes. She had to get away before he asked her what was wrong. As she pondered the best way to escape, a familiar engine sounded, saving her from having to explain.

"I think George and Emily are back." She climbed over Matt and got out of bed. Then she picked up her dress and panties from the floor, slipped them on as quickly as she could and headed for the kitchen to make herself look busy—and guilt free.

She got as far as the living room, where she glanced at her reflection in the glass doors of the antique hutch against the wall and rolled her eyes. Talk about the walk of shame. She'd been in such a hurry to waylay George and Emily before they came inside and found her and Matt in bed, that she hadn't realized her appearance would pretty much shout out what they'd been doing.

Why hadn't she taken the time to run a brush through her hair? George was going to suspect that they'd...

Her shoulders slumped, and she blew out a sigh. For some reason, she suspected that the man already knew what would happen when he took Emily for the afternoon.

Either way, she hastily combed her fingers through

her hair, then went to the kitchen, where she planned to look busy until they opened the back door.

After she washed her hands and took out the hamburger she'd let defrost in the fridge, they still hadn't come in to the house.

Curiosity got the better of her, and she went outside, in her bare feet no less, to see what they were up to.

When she spotted George unloading lumber, chicken wire and a small blue plastic kiddie pool from the back of his pickup, she froze in her steps.

A few feet away Emily sat on the ground, smiling as she peered into a cardboard box. Before Miranda could cross the yard to look inside and see what held her daughter's apt attention, Emily pulled out a little yellow duckling and pressed it gently to her cheek.

Oh, for Pete's sake. Miranda slapped her hands on her hips. "Emily Jane, I told you not to bring any more animals home."

"But I *didn't*. Uncle George is the one who bought them. I'm just going to take care of them for him."

"That's a fact," the old man said, nodding sagely. "I've always wanted to have a flock of ducks. I just never got around to getting any."

Yeah, right. Once Emily got a look at those cute little yellow balls of fluff at the feed store, George clearly hadn't had the heart to object. And now he was claiming they were his. And they would be, once she and Emily moved to their new place, especially if they ended up living within Brighton Valley's city limits.

"Guess what else we bought." Emily placed the duckling back into the box, scrambled to her feet and ran to the passenger side of the old pickup. After opening the door and reaching inside, she hurried to Miranda, carrying a DVD. "We went to Shop-Smart and found this."

The Wizard of Oz.

"Cool," Miranda said with a smile, but her eyes remained on the confined ducklings, which had begun to quack and scurry around the box.

After the conscientious duck-sitter hurried back to her little charges and told them she was back, she looked up at Miranda and smiled. "Uncle George and I already picked out names for them. Dorothy, Toto and Scarecrow."

Miranda rolled her eyes and muttered, "Ponies and doggies and ducks. Oh, my."

When the back door squeaked open, Miranda looked over her shoulder and watched Matt hobble outside, fresh from the shower and wearing his brace. He looked good. Refreshed. As if he'd just taken a nap. On the other hand, she was a wreck.

She glanced down at her dusty bare feet and slowly shook her head. She must look worse than she'd thought. Before taking a step in either direction, she raked her fingers through her messy hair, only to snag a nail on a snarl.

Great. Just great. Too bad she couldn't click her heels and zoom off to Kansas.

She turned and tossed Matt a weary don't-even-say-it smile. Then she headed for the house—and to the shower—wondering what George must think.

Before she reached the back door, she scolded herself for falling back on a bad habit.

In the past, when she'd been an unwed, pregnant teen, she'd worried way too much about what others thought, which was probably due to her father's concerns at the time. But she wasn't going to fall back into that self-deprecating trap anymore.

The only opinions that really mattered to her were Emily's and Matt's. As for her daughter, Emily adored Matt and would be thrilled if he and Miranda were to have an intimate relationship, assuming things continued in that direction.

That only left Matt and his thoughts about the future. And so far, as troubling as it was, he hadn't said a word.

After taking a long shower and shampooing her hair, Miranda slipped on a pair of comfy black stretch pants and a pink top. Then she grabbed her cell phone and padded to the overstuffed chair in her bedroom.

She'd put off calling her father long enough. And now that she and Matt had reconciled—at least, that seemed like a fair assumption for her to make—she wanted Matt to know that she wasn't afraid to level with her dad. She'd tell him where she was staying and who was sleeping down the hall. After he blew a fuse, she'd admit that she was pregnant and that she planned to relocate to Brighton Valley. He'd be hurt and angry, of course. But experience told her that it would be best if he blew off a little steam. And then, as usual, he'd get over it.

When she dialed his number, the call rolled over to voice mail. So she left a message. "It's me, Papa. I'll try you at the office."

Less than a minute later, Carolina Sanchez, one of several secretaries, answered the phone. "Contreras Farms."

"Hi, Caroline. This is Miranda. Is my father available?"

"No, I'm afraid not. He flew to Los Mochis yesterday to meet with Gavin's father and two other investors. From what I understand, the cell phone reception is pretty sketchy. I've already got a list of messages to give him once he's back on the grid."

"When do you expect him to return?" she asked.

"Maybe tonight or early tomorrow morning. But since the company jet is having a maintenance check, he'll have to fly home commercially. Can I give him a message?"

"No, I'll wait until he gets back to the States and contact him then."

After ending the call, Miranda went to the kitchen to fix spaghetti for dinner. She really didn't mind cooking. And she hated to see both Matt and George pick up meals to bring home, even if they both insisted they were used to doing that.

Two hours later, after they'd eaten dinner and she'd put the dishes into the dishwasher, she pulled out a couple of microwave popcorn packets from the pantry, as well as a liter of root beer from the fridge and a gallon of vanilla ice cream from the freezer.

"Whatcha doin'?" Emily asked, as she entered the kitchen.

"Getting ready for movie night."

"Are you going to eat that sweet stuff, too?"

"Of course."

Emily joined Miranda at the kitchen counter, then lifted a cupped hand to her mouth and whispered, "I don't want to hurt your feelings, but you've been getting a little fat. And my teacher said that happens when you eat too much sugar. Want me to get you something healthy to eat, like a cracker or an apple or something?"

Miranda fought a smile. She hadn't wanted to tell Emily about the baby until after she'd told her father. But since that phone call was as good as made, she turned to her daughter, her eyes glistening in mirth.

"Uh-oh," Emily said. "You're crying. I'm sorry. I didn't mean to hurt your feelings. I don't care if you get big and fat. I just thought Daddy might like you better if…"

She didn't finish what she meant to say, but she didn't need to.

"First of all," Miranda said, "the look and shape of our bodies doesn't have anything to do with the people we are on the inside. So if your father doesn't like me just the way I am, he can move on to someone else."

Emily's eyes widened. "But we don't want that to happen, right?"

Miranda laughed. "No, we really don't. But do you want to know a secret?"

When Emily nodded, she bent down to her daughter,

cupped her own hands and whispered, "There's a reason my tummy is getting big. I'm going to have a baby."

Emily gasped and her eyes widened. "Really?"

"Yes, it's true. You're going to have a little brother by the end of the summer."

A smile slid across her sweet face. "Getting a baby is going to be even better than getting a litter of puppies!"

Without a doubt. Especially considering all the furry little mouths they already had to feed.

"Does Daddy know?" she asked.

Miranda nodded. "I told him first."

Emily let out a gleeful shriek, then turned back toward the living room, where Matt was setting up the DVD.

"Guess what," she called out as she hurried away, her decibel level high with excitement. "I know the secret, too, Daddy."

As happy as Miranda was to get such an enthusiastic response from her daughter, and as relieved as she was to have the announcement behind her, she still had one more confession to make.

In spite of her belief that her father, in time, would accept the news, a slither of apprehension swirled around her.

What if she was wrong?

Last night, after the movie ended and the house grew quiet, Matt had been tempted to slip into Miranda's room so they could make love again, but he'd remained in his own bed, pondering an uncertain future.

It wasn't just the possibility of ending his career and the subsequent hit it would take on his livelihood that kept him tossing and turning until dawn. Even before he came home and found Miranda and Emily staying at the Double G, he'd known that it wouldn't be easy for him to give up the rodeo—should it come to that. And now that he had Miranda and the kids to think about, giving it all up—not just fame, travel and the thrill of competition, but the money—was going to be even harder.

Sure, he could go to work with Drew Madison, his friend and the head promoter at Esteban Enterprises. The job would be a good fit. And he didn't mind having to hobnob with wealthy Texas businessmen. But no matter how good Matt was at charming folks with his soft southern drawl and his fun-loving style, he didn't feel comfortable dressed in fancy Western wear, which would be expected of him.

No, he'd rather ride in the rodeo than take on the responsibility of talking people into sponsoring them.

Of course, taking on a family and becoming a good role model for two kids was one hell of a responsibility. And when push came to shove, it was one that he wasn't quite sure he was qualified to assume.

Either way, he'd made a promise he meant to keep, and he figured it would all work out. Somehow. That is, as long as Miranda's father didn't interfere.

Not that Matt was afraid of the man. Hell, that had never been the case. The biggest problem he had with Carlos Contreras was that the guy refused to accept Matt's value as a human being. And he doubted the man's opinion would change whether Matt continued to compete, took on the job as a promoter or if, God forbid, he went to work as a ranch hand for his uncle. Actually, if truth be told, even Matt thought Miranda deserved better than that.

For now, he'd have to shake those troubling thoughts and focus on the stuff he'd packed to take with him.

When he was convinced that he had everything he'd need for the next two days, he grabbed the canvas handle of the carry-on bag and headed for the back door.

He paused in the living room, where Emily was sitting on the floor in front of the TV, watching a cartoon. Sweetie Pie lay beside her, taking a nap.

"I'm leaving now," he said.

The dog momentarily looked up from its snooze, but the little girl was so captivated by the story on the screen that she must not have heard him.

"Emily?"

She turned away from the television. "Huh?"

"I'm going to Houston for a few days. Do you have a hug for me?"

She tore her gaze away from the cartoon long enough to reluctantly get up from the sofa, cross the room and open her arms.

Matt set down his bag, scooped her up and kissed her cheek. "Be good for your mom."

"Okay," she said. "I'm going to miss you."

He was going to miss her, too. After setting her back on the floor, he picked up his bag and limped to the kitchen, where the warm, sweet aroma of something freshly baked filled the air.

Miranda had been busy this morning. Several dozen chocolate chip cookies cooled on the racks she'd spread out on the counter. Her back was to him as she took another batch out of the oven.

It was a homey sight and smell he'd rarely—if ever—experienced. And one he found surprisingly appealing.

"Something sure smells good," he said.

She set down the potholder she'd been using and turned around with a smile. "Doesn't it?"

He nodded toward the service porch and the back door. "I'm taking off now."

"All right, but don't leave yet. I want to send some cookies with you. I'll make sure you'll have some to snack on while you drive and enough to share with everyone at the meeting. It'll just take me a minute. Then I'll bring them out to the truck."

He wasn't sure what he expected from her. A little more emotion, he supposed. Maybe a hug or a kiss goodbye.

But then again, maybe she planned to do that when she brought the cookies outside. So he shook off the brief sense of disappointment and limped to the door.

He'd no more than taken two steps outside, when a black luxury sedan drove up and screeched to a stop. The driver's door opened up and Carlos Contreras got out, his face red and fists clenched at his sides.

"Where's Miranda?" he asked.

Matt blew out a sigh. "In the house. But she's on her way out."

Carlos folded his arms across his chest and chuffed. "I couldn't believe it when Gavin told me she was here."

Matt cocked his head to the side. "How'd Gavin know where she was?"

"He's the one who hired a private investigator this time." Carlos shook his gray head in disgust. "You always were a bad influence on her. And now, thanks to you, she's been lying to me again."

Matt's first impulse was to defend himself. Miranda and Emily had been at the ranch more than two months before he'd gotten there. And if anything, he'd encouraged her to tell her father the truth. But he wasn't going to throw her under the bus.

Besides, if they wanted the world to think that he was the father of her baby, that they'd reconnected last year, during the holidays, then her father's assumption would help their story hold up.

Carlos slowly shook his head. "I can't believe this. She's been here all along. With a *friend*, she'd said. But she wouldn't tell me who. And now I know why."

Matt wasn't up for a confrontation. Nor did he feel good about leaving Miranda to deal with it on her own. He dropped his bag on the ground, wishing he could ditch his human burden as easily.

Carlos shook his head in disgust. "I suppose she just made up that story about Gavin hitting Emily as an excuse to cancel the wedding."

It took all Matt had not to roll his eyes. "There's no way Miranda would make up something up like that."

"So where is she?" Carlos asked. "Hiding? Like she's done for the past three months? Tell her to come outside. *Now.*"

"I'm not telling her anything. In case you haven't

noticed, she's an adult now. And she can make her own decisions."

Before Carlos could respond, Miranda stepped out the back door holding a plastic tub of cookies. When she spotted her father, she froze.

Carlos started toward her, scanning the length of her from the shock splashed across her face to her baby bump. At that point, he stopped mid-step and slapped his hands on his hips. "*Dios mio*. No wonder you didn't come home."

He was right about that. Matt waited for Miranda to respond, but she just stood there. Stunned, it would seem.

Carlos turned his fiery gaze on Matt. "What kind of man are you? Getting her pregnant twice?"

Now it was Matt's turn to hold his tongue, but only because he wanted to get a grip on his anger before he blew a head gasket.

"I've heard all about *you*." Carlos scrunched his face and let out a string of words in Spanish, most likely obscenities. "And I've read about your sexual exploits."

Matt had had several lovers over the years, and he'd heard the stories, too. But most of them were exaggerated. "You shouldn't believe everything you read."

"Have you no shame?" Carlos asked. "No honor? Where have you been for the past eight years?"

At that, Matt threw up his hands. Miranda's old man would never approve of him, no matter how many bulls he rode, how many buckles he won. And Matt wasn't going to stand here and argue with him. Besides, if he didn't leave now, he'd probably end up throttling the guy.

"I hate to run out on the family reunion," he said, "but I've had enough fun for the day."

As he turned toward his pickup, Miranda called out, "Matt! Wait up!"

He stopped, but only to say, "Don't bother, Miranda."

She set the cookies aside and started down the steps. "Just listen to me. I don't care what my father says or what he thinks. We're a family now."

"No," Matt said, "you're wrong. Your father and I will never be family. So choose me. Or choose him. But you can't have us both."

She pondered his ultimatum a beat too long.

"It's over," he said. "I'll never desert my daughter, but there's no way in hell things will ever work out for you and me."

As she started to cross the yard, he shook his head, silently telling her to back off. He needed space. And time to think.

What he didn't need was to hang around and take her dad's insults and then wait for her to acquiesce to the old man's demands, no matter how badly the rebel in him wanted to stand his ground. Or how badly his heart ached at her rejection.

As he limped toward his truck, he spotted George standing in the open doorway of the barn. He'd probably heard everything, but what the hell.

George followed him out to his pickup.

"You just gonna run off like a stubborn, broken-hearted fool?" his uncle asked.

Matt rolled his eyes. "Lay off me. I have a meeting in Houston. And my leaving has nothing to do with a broken heart. It just makes good sense. I'm not going to have a relationship with Miranda. Not while Carlos still has a hold on her."

"Men like him usually back down when challenged."

Matt would have stood up to him, but Carlos had a rapid-fire temper, and it wouldn't take much for Matt to double up his fists and let the old man have it. Besides, Emily's cartoon movie couldn't last forever. She'd come looking for cookies or something. And if she heard any commotion outside, she'd come out to see what was going on.

What would a confrontation between her father and grandfather do to her? Scar her for life, no doubt.

Matt reached into his pocket and whipped out his keys. "Since you enjoy having Miranda and Emily here, you're the one who should go back there and give him your two cents. I couldn't care less."

"I ain't the one who's lying." George narrowed his eyes as if making a silent accusation.

"Neither am I. Miranda's the one who hasn't been honest."

George folded his arms across his chest. "I beg to differ."

"When was I ever dishonest with her?" Certainly not nine years ago, when he'd worn his heart on his sleeve. And not this time around, either.

"I never said you lied to Miranda. You've been lying

to *yourself* for years about the feelings you've always had for her."

Matt merely shook his head and climbed into his pickup, his knee hurting, his heart heavy and his mind made up.

Tears stung Miranda's eyes as she watched Matt drive away. She wanted nothing more than to run to him and beg him to come back. But that wasn't going to solve anything. Not when what he'd said was true. Not when she already knew what she needed to do.

Choose me. Or choose him. But you can't have us both.

Only trouble was, she loved and wanted both men in her life. And there didn't seem to be an easy solution.

Her father shook his head in disgust. "There he goes. Ditching you and his responsibilities."

"What did you expect?" she launched back at him. "I don't blame him for leaving. Rather than ever giving him a chance, you've been mean and unreasonable."

He rolled his eyes. "You're just like your mother, ready to run off with the first man who says you're pretty."

She knew he'd apologize to her later, but the cruel accusation still lanced deep into her heart.

In typical cowboy fashion, George stepped up to defend her honor. "Listen," he said. "Miranda might be your daughter, but you'll speak to her with the utmost respect when I'm around and when you're on my property."

"If she'll get into my car, we'll take our troubles with us."

"I'm not going anywhere with you," Miranda said.

She wasn't a little girl anymore. Matt had been right about that, too.

"You belong in San Antonio. And so does Emily. She has everything she needs in the city."

"Emily is happy here," Miranda said. "I'm going to sell the condo and find a place in this area where she can raise her animals."

"You want to live on a ranch?" He clicked his tongue, then started toward her as if he could actually force her to do something against her will.

"Step away from her," George said. "Don't make me call the sheriff."

Miranda hoped and prayed that Emily would remain in the house watching TV. Because things were sure to escalate between the two stubborn old men.

But when George paled, clutched his chest and dropped to his knees, she forgot about her concern for her daughter and rushed to his side.

Chapter Twelve

Miranda's fingers trembled as she dialed 9-1-1.

"This can't be happening," she muttered as she waited for someone to answer.

Seconds later, the dispatcher did. "9-1-1, what's your emergency?"

"We need an ambulance at the Double G Ranch on Oakdale Road in Brighton Valley. George Grimes collapsed. I think he's having a heart attack."

Her father, who'd frozen in stunned silence, eased closer. "What can I…?"

Miranda waved him off, as she provided the information the dispatcher requested. "He's seventy-two. He's avoided doctors in the past, but he's seen one recently. I'm not sure who it was or why he went. He wouldn't talk to me about it."

Oh, God. Just send the ambulance. We can talk about this stuff later.

She glanced down at George, who lay on the ground, his eyes closed, his skin ashen and clammy, his chest rising and falling.

But too fast? Too slow?

"Is that ambulance on the way?" she asked.

"Yes," the dispatcher said. "Is he conscious and breathing?"

"Conscious? I'm not sure. But he's breathing."

"Do you know CPR?" the man asked.

"Yes. At least, I've had classes. And I know not to do it unless he stops breathing. But please tell the paramedics to hurry." She looked at George again, but this time his chest wasn't moving. "Oh, God. I think he stopped breathing."

"Don't hang up. I'll stay on the line while you begin CPR."

As instructed, Miranda set aside the phone without ending the call and began to pump George's chest, hoping that she remembered everything she'd learned during her health class in college. She swore she'd take a refresher first aid course as soon as she could find one.

Her father circled George, then dropped to his knees and looked at her with apologetic eyes. "What can I do to help?"

Seriously? He'd been enough help already.

Between the breaths she blew into George's mouth, and the two-handed pumps she pressed to his chest, she said, "You stay here. And watch Emily. I'm going to follow the paramedics to the hospital."

"Of course, *mija*. No problem."

Miranda returned her full attention to George, praying her efforts weren't in vain, that the paramedics would arrive in time and that George would be back to his sweet, gruff and rascally self in no time at all.

All the while, she continued to perform CPR until the ambulance arrived, lights flashing, siren blasting. It seemed as if it had taken them forever, but in reality, it was probably only five or ten minutes.

As she moved away from George, allowing the paramedics to take over, her father pulled her aside.

"I'm sorry," he said.

How typical. Blow up first, then think about the situation, realize he'd overreacted and apologize.

"You *should* be sorry," she said. "This didn't need to happen. Just look at that man. All he wanted to do was defend me."

"Mija." His brow furrowed. "You're looking at me like I'm a monster."

"Sometimes you act like one." She crossed her arms and lifted her chin. "You've never been physically abusive, but your anger, harsh words and knee-jerk reactions can be hurtful and, sometimes, that can be far more damaging than a smack in the face."

He blew out a sigh. "I love you, honey. And all I've ever tried to do was look out for you. And for Emily."

"That may be true, but you aren't looking out for me and my best interests when you try to control my thoughts, feelings and plans for my life. That's grossly unfair. You might call it love, but if you *truly* cared about me, you'd first ask me what I want, what I like, how I feel. But that never seems to matter."

His shoulders slumped.

Miranda didn't stand up to her father very often, but doing so today gave her a burst of confidence, a feeling of power.

She shot a glance at George, who still lay on the ground but seemed to be stirring. The CPR had stopped, and one of the paramedics was inserting an IV. Thank God. He was breathing again, but she suspected he wasn't out of the woods yet.

She left her father and hurried to George. Afraid to get in the way of the paramedics, she still managed to hover over him and say, "You gave us a good scare."

The old man attempted a half-hearted smile.

When one of the paramedics indicated that she should take a step back, she returned to her father's side and, with her eyes glued to the medical drama unfolding, spoke to her dad. "You probably don't know this or even care, but I didn't want to become a CPA. I would have rather gone into teaching. But I gave in to you out of appreciation for all you did for me when I was growing up. But what's wrong with me having my own dreams and following my heart? Wouldn't allowing me to choose my own path be a better way for you to show your love and respect for me?"

"I'm sorry," he said again.

"Sometimes being sorry doesn't help." She stood tall and held her head high.

"I'd like to make things better," he said. "I didn't realize how much you cared about Matt and his uncle."

"Papa, they're part of my family, too. George is the uncle I never had. And believe it or not, I love Matt Grimes even more today than I did nine years ago. You might have thought you were protecting me back then, by forcing me to break up with him, but it tore me up inside. Still, I went along with your demands when I should have run away from home and married him as soon as I turned eighteen."

Her father seemed to think on that. Finally, he said, "Why *didn't* you run away?"

"Maybe I just wanted to make up for the way my mom left you. But now I realize, at least in part, why she made the decision she did. Sometimes you can be a tyrant."

Her father lowered his head. "In some ways, you might be right. She left me for someone else, a man who could give her more than I could. I got over what she did to me, but I never forgave her for leaving you. And I tried to make up for it the only way I knew how."

"You need to put her rejection and the past behind you, like I've been able to do. That is, until you throw her in my face and tell me I'm just like her. But I'm not at all like her." Miranda placed her hand on her baby bump. "I'd never give up my children and let someone else raise them."

"I know you won't."

Miranda studied her father, noted his growing remorse. "I've always known how angry you are at my mother, and that you've let those bitter feelings take root inside you. So when you accuse me of being just like her, it hurts worse than you can ever imagine."

"I never meant to lash out at you like that," he said.

"But you did."

Miranda glanced at the paramedics, saw them loading George onto a gurney. Thank God the dear old man was stable enough to transport to the hospital.

"We can talk more later," she told her father. "I'm going to have to leave now. But there's something you need to know. Like it or not, I'm selling my condo and moving to Brighton Valley. And I'm going to marry Matt Grimes, unless you chased him off for good."

"Are you sure about that?" he asked.

"About my decisions? Absolutely."

"I mean about Matt leaving for good."

Her heart bent into itself, and she did her best to recover. "I guess that's left to be seen. Either way, if you don't seek therapy and get into some anger management classes, you won't see me or the kids very often. I love Emily and this new little boy with all my heart and soul. And I'll be damned if I'll let you talk to them the way you talk to me."

Then, while her father pondered her threat, she went into the house to get her purse and her car keys.

All the while, her heart ached and her gut clenched. Losing Matt for the second time threatened to be her undoing. But whether she and Matt reconciled or not, George would always be a part of her family, and she'd do whatever she could for him for as long as he lived.

As Matt barreled down the interstate on his way to Houston, he tightened his grip on the steering wheel and swore under his breath. He'd meant everything he'd said to Miranda back at the ranch. He'd had his fill of her father and never wanted to lay eyes on him again. And if that meant he had to sever ties with Miranda, then so be it.

Only trouble was, he'd never turn his back on Emily. That's why he planned to see an attorney while he was in Houston. He was going to need someone to help him get a court order granting him visitation and securing his legal rights as Emily's father.

Carlos would probably pitch a fit, and who knew what Miranda might think, but he didn't care.

His cell phone rang, and when Miranda's number flashed on the screen, he let it roll to voice mail. He was too raw to talk to her now, too angry.

Less than three minutes later, she called again. But he still wasn't ready to talk to her and just let it ring.

But that didn't stop her from calling again.

And again.

Dammit. He'd told her to back off. Maybe not in words, but he'd let her know he needed to put some distance between them. Apparently, she didn't care about giving him the space and time he needed.

He finally answered, just so she'd stop calling, but he didn't open with *Hello* or a cheery tone.

"There's nothing to talk about," he said. At least, not until after a process server handed her the documents from family court.

"George is headed to Brighton Valley Medical Center," she said. "He's in an ambulance, and I'm following behind it."

His heart sank, his anger fizzled and his foot eased off the gas pedal. "What happened?"

"I think he had a heart attack. I won't know for sure until I get a chance to talk to the doctors. I'll let you know what they say."

Did she think he was going to continue on to Houston after getting news like that? "I'm making a U-turn. I'll meet you at the hospital."

"Okay."

He expected her to end the call, but she didn't. And neither did he. For some reason, he wanted to keep the line open.

Because of his uncle, of course. Yet, as much as he hated to admit it, something else made him hang on. Because right this minute, he'd never felt so alone or so far away.

"Miranda?" he asked.

"Yes?"

"Thanks." He waited a couple of beats before he finally disconnected the line. He could call her back if he needed to. And he knew that she'd answer.

He spotted a safe place to turn around up ahead. Once he was back on the road and headed in the right direction, he drove as fast as the law would allow.

With each passing mile, thoughts began to plague him, each one coming at him in single images and in short phrases, snapping in his mind, the cadence like that of a Vegas dealer with a deck of cards, each one flashing before him face up.

George could die...

Or end up an invalid...

I could lose the only family I've ever had...

A family that almost included Miranda and the kids.

That is, until Matt had tossed her aside like a bad hand of cards, losing her all over again. And losing her for good.

Or had he? He'd just gotten off the phone with her. And she'd called him several times, pursuing him.

Of course, she'd only done that so she could tell him about George. She, more than anyone, knew how he felt about his uncle, and as a courtesy...

No, it was more than that.

Matt, wait up.

I don't care what my father says or what he thinks. We're a family now.

She was right. It'd begun years ago, when a lonely old rancher, a rebellious throwaway kid and the young girl who'd loved them all turned to each other, becoming a family of sorts.

They still were, he supposed. Some ties weren't easily severed, although Matt had taken a pretty good slice at them today.

And somehow, he had to make things right.

It wouldn't be easy, though. Not the way he'd gotten used to handling life's ups and downs. In the past, whenever faced with an awkward or trying situation, he'd just shake it off and go to the next rodeo. Bull riding and the cheer of the crowd had been his fix. And for the past eight or nine years, that fix had been the only thing that mattered to him.

However, that wasn't the case anymore. Making love

with Miranda had changed things. And as a result, it had changed *him*.

But had it changed him enough to challenge Miranda's father, to claim the family he wanted, the family that always should have been his?

All Matt knew was that he had to get to the hospital before it was too late.

Nearly twenty minutes later, Matt arrived at the Brighton Valley Medical Center. After parking his truck, he hurried to the Emergency Department entrance. Once inside the waiting room, he scanned the sea of people seated in chairs—a woman holding a bloodied towel to a child's head, a red-eyed man coughing into his sleeve.

This was no place for a pregnant woman to be waiting, but he figured Miranda would be here. The minute he spotted her, he let out a sigh of relief and headed toward the registration desk, where she stood, haggard with worry and grief. She was a welcome sight—and still the prettiest woman he'd ever seen.

His heart cramped, and as much as he'd have liked to hang onto his anger, his resentment, it all seemed to pale when compared to the things that really mattered.

"How's he doing?" Matt asked.

She tucked a strand of hair behind her ear. "I'm not sure. The doctor said he was conscious, but we can't see him yet. He told me where I could find the family waiting room. It's located near the cardiac unit, but I thought I should stay put until you got here. And now that you are, we can go together."

The hard facts began to snap like cards again.

Family...

Together.

He was tempted to reach for her hand, to bind them together, but he kept his arms at his sides and said, "Let's go."

As he limped down the corridor with her, following the signs and arrows pointing to the cardiac unit, he asked, "Where's Emily?"

"I left her with my dad."

Matt stiffened, and his fists began to clench, but he shook off the negative reaction that would undoubtedly set the clock back an hour earlier, to the time he'd confronted the old man. Besides, under the circumstances, that was Miranda's only option—other than staying at the ranch with their daughter or bringing Emily here.

Hospitals could be a scary place. And on top of that, if George didn't make it—*God, please don't take him yet*—Emily would be devastated.

No, she was better off at home.

"Just so you know," Miranda said, "my dad was pretty remorseful when I left."

Matt held back the retort that formed on the tip of his tongue.

"After you drove away, I told him that I was moving to Brighton Valley no matter what. And that you were going to be a big part of Emily's life." She paused, then added, "Mine, too—assuming that's okay with you."

A flood of emotions, relief only one of them, settled over him. He hadn't chased her away. And while she hadn't mentioned living together or anything legally binding, it'd be pretty darn hard to be a *big* part of her life if they didn't make some kind of commitment.

"It's more than okay," he said, as they continued down the corridor, "but if it's all the same to you, I'll make sure I'm gone whenever your dad comes to visit." He hoped she wouldn't object to his comment, but he wasn't about to roll over and accept her father's words and opinions as gospel.

"I don't think that'll be necessary. I also told my dad that he needed to get his anger under control because if he didn't get professional help, he wasn't going to be a very big part of our lives."

Matt blew out a sigh, glad she'd finally taken a stand. "How'd he take it?"

"Like I said, he was pretty contrite and quiet when I left."

As happy as Matt was to hear that, her father wasn't the only one who had to deal with his anger and hard feelings. "I'm sorry for blowing up and running off like I did. I wasn't up for a fight with your dad, especially since I was afraid Emily might come outside and witness a lot of yelling and harsh words. But I should have kept my cool, even if he didn't."

Miranda reached for his arm and pulled him to a halt in the middle of the hospital corridor. "And just for the record, I wrapped up my speech by letting my dad know that I choose *you*, Matt. I'll always put you first."

As their gazes met and locked, the love shining in her eyes chased away any lingering anger he might have been harboring and every painful memory he'd ever had.

"I choose you, too," he said. "I have no idea how things will work out—with George, my knee, the rodeo or your dad—but I love you, Miranda. I always have and always will. We've spent so many damned years apart, and now that we finally have a chance to be together, I'm not letting you go. Marry me, Miranda."

She tossed him a heart-strumming smile, her eyes bright and glistening with what could only be happy tears. "I'm definitely willing."

Before sweeping her into his arms and kissing her, he asked, "What are the chances of us pulling together a wedding before the baby comes? I want my name on his birth certificate. That way, there won't be any doubt about who his father is."

"I'd say the chances are excellent." A happy tear slid down her dimpled cheek. "Our son is going to be one lucky baby."

"And I'm one lucky guy." Matt brushed a kiss over her lips, then he continued to hold her close, to savor the feel of her in his arms and bask in the sweet smell of sugar, vanilla and chocolate that still clung to her hair and clothes.

If he'd ever wondered what a real home and family felt like, this was it. Miranda was it.

On those long hard days, when he felt broken and tired, the only place he wanted to be was wrapped in her arms, heart to heart.

"I could really get used to coming home to you," he said. "So much so, that I'm not sure I want to follow the rodeo circuit any more. Not if it means long absences."

"I hate to admit it," she said, "but I'd really miss you

when you're gone. And so would the kids But we can talk more about that later, after we find out how George is doing."

He took her by the hand, and they continued to the family waiting room, the soles of their shoes clicking upon the tile floor.

Just as they reached the door, a doctor met them in the hallway, and Miranda introduced them.

"Dr. Kipper," she said, "this is Matt Grimes, George's nephew."

As the men shook hands, Matt asked, "How's he doing?"

"Much better. We're still running tests, but there doesn't seem to be any long-term damage to his heart. We're going to keep him here for a few days, and it looks like he'll need a stent. But it's nothing we can't fix."

"When can we see him?" Miranda asked.

"Not for an hour or so. But I'm almost afraid to let him know you're here. He's been asking to go home, and he's giving the nursing staff a hard time, insisting they bring him his britches."

Matt laughed. "Sounds like he's going to be just fine. But don't worry. Once we get a chance to visit him, we'll insist that he stay here until he's on the mend."

"That's good to know," the doctor said.

"In the meantime," Miranda added, "you can tell him that Matt and I will let him help plan our wedding if he settles down and doesn't give the nurses any more trouble."

"Do you think that'll work?" the doctor asked.

"Without a doubt." Matt slipped his arm around Miranda, pulled her to his side and smiled. "He's been waiting years to hear news like that."

"Good," the doctor said. "There's nothing that makes my job easier than a happy patient."

As Dr. Kipper walked down the hall, Matt and Miranda made their way into the family waiting room.

"This may sound weird," he said, "but as bad as this day has been—the blowup with your dad, the news about George, the worry of it all—it's helped me to realize something important."

"What's that?"

"It's not blood ties that create a family. It's love. And as long as I have you and the kids, nothing else matters. Not a knee injury, not the rodeo and not even your dad."

She pulled him to another halt, threw her arms around his neck and drew his lips to hers, letting him know they were a team—friends and lovers for life.

George remained in the hospital for several days before coming home. Once he was settled in his own room, he'd told Miranda, "You don't need to take care of me. You already have your hands full, and I don't want to be a burden."

"But I want to be here," she'd told him, placing a kiss on his brow.

Since then, he'd been a real sweetheart. That is, until the opening day of the Rocking Chair Rodeo rolled around, and Miranda told him that she and Matt had hired a nurse from a home health care agency to stay with him at the ranch while she, Matt and Emily were gone.

"That was a damn fool thing to do," George said, grimacing as he tried to get out of bed. "And a complete waste of good money when I'm perfectly capable of taking care of myself."

Miranda placed a gentle hand on his shoulder, carefully pressing him back down on the mattress. "I know that, but we'd all feel better if we didn't leave you alone."

The tough old rancher grumbled and swore under his breath. "I'm not used to folks fussin' over me."

"You'd better get used to it," Miranda told him. "I'm going to need you fit as a fiddle by the time the baby comes. You're going to have to help me with little Georgie."

"Georgie?" he asked, his voice and his expression softening in unison.

At one time, she'd thought about naming the baby after her father, but she'd changed her mind the day Uncle George stood up to her dad.

"That's right," she said. "You have a namesake. We're going to call him George Matthew Grimes."

"No kidding?" The roughened old cowboy's eyes watered.

She nodded, as she rested her hand on her baby bump. "Since we'd rather not get married until the doctor says that you can attend, we'd all be disappointed if there was a setback in your recovery because you pushed yourself too hard."

George snorted. "All right. I'll stay home and take it easy. But I still don't need a nurse."

He continued to scowl and complain for the next couple of hours. That is, until he laid eyes on the nurse, an attractive forty-something brunette with big blue eyes and feminine curves that could rock a pair of pale green scrubs.

"My name is Jolene," the nurse said, extending a manicured hand to her patient.

"George Grimes," he said, offering her a big ol' smile and giving her hand a shake.

Miranda had to stifle a chuckle.

But she just about lost it when George said, "Now that Jolene's here, you guys had better get a move on. That rodeo is going to start soon, and they expect a big crowd. You don't want to be late."

Twenty minutes later, they arrived at the county fairgrounds and found the parking lot nearly full.

George had been right. People were already filling the grandstands and lining up at the concession booths.

"The bigshots at Esteban Enterprises have to be happy about this crowd," Miranda said to Matt, as Emily skipped beside them, her ponytail swishing across her back.

"I'm sure Drew Madison is thrilled. I haven't seen him yet, but he's here somewhere. And he's probably eager to talk to me."

Miranda knew why. When Drew learned that Matt had decided to end his bull-riding career, he offered him a job, and Matt told them he'd have to think about it.

"Have you made a decision yet?" she asked.

"Yes, but it's not what they're going to want to hear. Working for them would still require me to travel, and I'd rather stick closer to home. Besides, the doctor told George he'd better think about retirement. And I'd like to buy the ranch from him."

"I can't see that man sitting in a rocker all day. What would he do if he retired?"

Matt laughed. "Well, since he'd be a permanent resident at the Double G, I expect he'd follow me around all day and tell me what I should be doing differently."

"Do you really want to run cattle?" she asked. "Not that it would matter to me. But you never wanted to before."

"Actually, I'd rather raise rodeo stock. I have a lot of connections, and that would keep me in the thick of things, but I'd still be home for dinner most nights."

"Speaking of connections," she said, "it certainly looks as though your endorsement and personal promotional efforts were a success. Thanks in large part to you, both the Rocking Chair Ranch and Kidville will get sizable checks."

"I'm glad. They're both great charities and will put the money to good use."

"Emily," Miranda called to their daughter, who'd skipped a little too far ahead. "You'd better get back here before you lose us."

When she didn't respond, Matt released Miranda's hand and went after their daughter and brought her back.

"They're selling snacks," Emily said. "Can I have a popcorn? And a lemonade?"

"Okay," Matt said. "But first, I want to introduce

you both to Jim Hoffman, one of the directors of Kidville. I just spotted him on the grassy area near the front entrance."

A short walk and a minute later, Matt introduced Miranda to a round-faced heavyset man in his mid- to late-fifties.

"Jim," he said, "this is Miranda Contreras, my soon-to-be wife and the CPA I told you about. And this is our daughter, Emily."

Jim took Miranda's hand, his nearly swallowing hers up, and gave it a warm and gentle squeeze. "I'm so happy to meet you. If you have time next week, I'd like you to come to Kidville and talk to my wife and me about going to work for us. Matt says you might have something else lined up, but we could sure use someone to conduct an audit before long."

"I do have a couple of irons in the fire," Miranda admitted. "But I'd be happy to help with that audit. I'd also like to stop by and see you next week. I've heard wonderful things about Kidville and the work you two have done."

"That sounds like a plan," Jim said. "It was nice meeting you, but you'll have to excuse me. I need to look for my wife before she and the kids we brought with us find seats without me."

"And I have to find a seat before my knee gives out on me," Matt said. But he'd hardly turned toward the grandstand when he said, "Uh-oh. Getting off our feet will have to wait." He pointed toward a parade of senior citizens, all men wearing Western wear and cowboy hats. Several rode in wheelchairs, and a couple pushed walkers.

An older cowboy, who still stood tall and strong, pushed one of the wheelchairs, while an attractive redhead in her sixties pushed another.

"Looks like Sam and Joy, the couple who run the Rocking Chair Ranch, have brought some of the retired cowboys with them. I'd better say hello."

Miranda smiled to herself. One step forward, two steps back.

Moments later, Matt was introducing her to Sam and Joy.

"What'd you do?" Matt asked. "Rent a bus?"

"Just about," Sam said. "Joy and I both drove, but we wouldn't have been able to fit everyone who was able to attend into our cars. So some of the ladies from the Brighton Valley Women's Club offered to help out."

"Maybe, after you get the funds from the rodeo, you'll be able to afford to buy a van."

"That's the plan," Sam said.

"Hey, Sam!" one of the old men said. "If you don't quit your yappin', we're going to miss the opening ceremony."

Sam laughed. "I've got a rebellion on my hands. So I'd better go."

As he and the old cowboys headed toward the stands, Miranda gave Matt's hand a tug. "And you'd better sit down."

"You got that right."

But before they made any forward progress at all,

Matt paused and pointed toward the entrance with his free hand. "Look who's here."

When she spotted her dad, her breath caught. "I didn't expect to see him show up."

"Neither did I."

Her father headed toward them, looking solemn—but not angry.

"Abuelito!" Emily, who'd just realized her grandfather had arrived, darted toward him, clearly happy to see him. He stooped to greet her with a smile and a hug, followed by a kiss on the cheek.

When Emily took her grandfather by the hand and led him to her parents, he said, "I hoped I'd find you here."

"What's up?" Miranda asked.

"I need to apologize," he told Matt. "But under the circumstances, saying 'I'm sorry' doesn't seem adequate."

Maybe not, but it was a start.

"I also want you to know that I'm turning over a new leaf. It might not be easy. Old habits are hard to break, but I'm sure going to try. I've already met with an anger management counselor, and I like her. I'm going to see her again next week."

"Thank you," Miranda said, glad that he'd listened, that he'd followed through.

"I wasn't sure when you two were getting married," her dad added. "All Miranda said was *soon*, so I wanted to make sure I got an invitation."

"We're getting married at the Brighton Valley Community Church at two o'clock next Saturday," Matt said. "It'll be a small wedding, since we don't want to wait any longer than we have to."

"I hope you'll be there," Miranda said.

"I wouldn't miss it, *mija*."

"Good." Miranda gave her father a hug. He held onto her a bit longer than she'd expected, but she could sense his repentance in the embrace. When he finally let her go, he managed a sheepish smile.

Then he turned to Matt. "How's your uncle?"

"He's at home, recovering. But he looks good and says he feels better than he has in years. We would have gotten married already, but we both want him to be there."

"I'm not going to be a flower girl," Emily said. "I get to be a bridesmaid. And tomorrow, Mom and I are going shopping to buy my dress."

"I can't wait to see you wearing it," he said. "You're going to be as pretty as your mama."

Emily reached for her grandfather's hand, then looked at Matt. "Can we get the lemonade now? I've been waiting a long time."

"And patiently," Matt said. "So yes, let's go."

With her free hand, she reached for her daddy, joining the men with her love and innocence, rather than the animosity that had separated them for years.

"By the way," Miranda's father said. "I'm moving the main office back to Brighton Valley. I figure you'll probably want to stay home with the baby after he's born, but your job will be ready for you when he gets older."

"Thanks. I appreciate that. But we'll have to see what happens."

Her father tilted his head, no doubt surprised by her comment.

"Just so you aren't blindsided," she said, "I've been talking to Hazel Jorgenson, the owner of the Brighton Valley Pharmacy. I want to help her get the soda fountain up and running again. We think we can turn it into a local landmark."

Her father blinked, clearly surprised by her plan, but he didn't object. And after a couple of beats, he said, "I hope things work out for you."

As they neared the concession stand, Miranda's father surprised her yet again.

"Emily," he said, "college has always been important to me. I know it's still a long time off for you, but I've set up educational trusts for you and your little brother so the money will be there for you. But if either or both of you decide you'd rather take another career path, I'll support your decisions."

Miranda's eyes filled with tears, something that seemed to be happening a lot lately, and she mouthed a silent *Thank you* to the first man she'd ever loved.

"The trust is flexible," her father said. "That means you can use the money to buy a house or start a business instead."

"I'm *definitely* going to college," Emily said. "I have to because I'm going to be a veterinarian. So I can use the money for that. But if there's any left over, can I use it for my rescue center?"

"You bet you can, *mija*. I had no idea you liked animals so much, even when you introduced me to all the ones living on the ranch."

"I *love* them. And guess what? Tomorrow my daddy is taking me to buy another lamb. Remember when I showed you Bob and told you I wanted to get him a wife? Well, it's going to be a girl lamb, and I'm going to name her Betty. Then they can have babies."

Her grandfather laughed. "I guess it's a good thing that you live on a ranch and not in the city."

"Yep." Emily released both of the men's hands so she could get in line.

Miranda couldn't believe the way her life had finally fallen into place. Sure, there were bound to be trials and setbacks. But nothing that love and family couldn't overcome.

She eased toward Matt and slipped her hand in his. "Have I told you how much I love you?"

He pulled her into his arms. "A couple of times, but not nearly enough."

Then he kissed her—right then and there, for all the world to see.

Epilogue

On Saturday afternoon, Matt stood beside the altar at the Brighton Valley Community Church in black jeans, a white Western shirt and a bolo tie, waiting for his bride to walk down the aisle. His old high school buddies, Clay Masters and Adam Santiago, stood with him—best men in every sense of the words.

Uncle George took a seat of honor in the front row, across from the pew where Miranda's father would sit after giving his daughter to Matt.

George obviously couldn't be happier to see the two people he loved the most in the world finally tie the knot. In fact, last night, he'd surprised them both by giving them a quitclaim deed to the ranch—his wedding gift to them.

"The only thing I'm not deeding over to you is my

bedroom," George had said. "Because I aim to live on the Double G until I die—or until you move me to the Rocking Chair Ranch.

"That's a promise," Matt told him.

Matt had invited his father and stepmother to attend the wedding, something Miranda had encouraged him to do. It hadn't taken much prodding, though. After all, this was the time for family harmony, forgiveness and second chances. His dad actually seemed pleased to hear the news and congratulated him.

"We'd be happy to attend," his dad had said. "But we're leaving on a cruise the night before. Can I make it up to you by taking you and Miranda to dinner when we get back?"

"Sure," Matt told him.

Because of his father's absence, Clay's wife Erica sat beside George. Next to her was her sister Elena and Drew Madison, Elena's husband.

Adam's wife Julie, who was a music therapist and a whiz on just about any instrument imaginable, sat at the church piano. As she began to play the wedding march, signaling that the bride would soon walk down the aisle, Matt's heart soared in anticipation. It had been a long, nine year wait, but Miranda would soon be his wife.

Emily, who wore a pretty yellow dress and held a bouquet of daisies, began to walk toward the altar first. Her bright-eyed smile and dimpled grin just about turned Matt inside out. But when he spotted the pregnant brunette walking behind her, his breath caught. Miranda, the love of his life, the mother of his children.

His eyes grew misty. Damn. He wasn't a softy. He

never cried. But this was different. *Today* was different. He'd never felt so many powerful, nearly overwhelming emotions—love, happiness, pride, hope....

Carlos smiled as he handed over his daughter's hand, clearly—finally—accepting Matt into his family—and finding him to be a man worthy of his daughter.

As Matt and Miranda turned to face the minister, Matt squeezed Miranda's hand, letting her know that they were bound together.

Not just for this moment, but forever.

* * * * *

Look for these titles from
USA TODAY *bestselling author Judy Duarte's*
Rocking Chair Rodeo miniseries

The Soldier's Twin Surprise
The Lawman's Convenient Family

Available now wherever
Harlequin Special Edition books
and ebooks are sold.

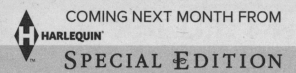

COMING NEXT MONTH FROM

HARLEQUIN®

SPECIAL EDITION

Available June 18, 2019

#2701 HER FAVORITE MAVERICK

Montana Mavericks: Six Brides for Six Brothers • by Christine Rimmer

Logan Crawford might just be the perfect man. A girl would have to be a fool to turn him down. Or a coward. Sarah Turner thinks she might be both. But the single mom has no time for love. Logan, however, is determined to steal her heart!

#2702 A PROMISE FOR THE TWINS

The Wyoming Multiples • by Melissa Senate

Former soldier Nick Garroway is in Wedlock Creek to fulfill a promise made to a fallen soldier: check in on the woman the man had left pregnant with twins. Brooke Timber is in need of a nanny, so what else can Nick do but fill in? She's also planning her father's wedding, and all the family togetherness soon has Brooke and Nick rethinking if this promise is still temporary.

#2703 THE FAMILY HE DIDN'T EXPECT

The Stone Gap Inn • by Shirley Jump

Dylan Millwright's bittersweet homecoming gets a whole lot sweeter when he meets Abby Cooper. But this mother of two is all about "the ties that bind," and Dylan isn't looking for strings to keep him down. But do this bachelor's wandering ways conceal the secretly yearning heart of a family man?

#2704 THE DATING ARRANGEMENT

Something True • by Kerri Carpenter

Is the bride who fell on top of bar owner Jack Wright a sign from above? But event planner Emerson Dewitt isn't actually a bride—much to her mother's perpetual disappointment. Until Jack proposes an arrangement. He'll pose as Emerson's boyfriend in exchange for her help relaunching his business. It's a perfect partnership. Until all that fake dating turns into very real feelings...

#2705 A FATHER FOR HER CHILD

Sutter Creek, Montana • by Laurel Greer

Widow Cadence Grigg is slowly putting her life back together—and raising her infant son. By her side is her late husband's best friend, Zach Cardenas, who can't help his burgeoning feelings for Cadie and her baby boy. Though determined not to fall in love again, Cadie might find that Cupid has other plans for her happily-ever-after...

#2706 MORE THAN ONE NIGHT

Wildfire Ridge • by Heatherly Bell

A one-night stand so incredible, Jill Davis can't forget. Memories so delectable, they sustained Sam Hawker through his final tour. Three years later, Jill is unexpectedly face-to-face with her legendary marine lover. And it's clear their chemistry is like gas and a match. Except Sam is her newest employee. That means hands off, sister! Except maybe...just this once? Ooh-rah!

YOU CAN FIND MORE INFORMATION ON UPCOMING HARLEQUIN® TITLES, FREE EXCERPTS AND MORE AT WWW.HARLEQUIN.COM.

HSECNM0619

*Former soldier Nick Garroway is in Wedlock Creek
to fulfill a promise made to a fallen soldier: check in
on the woman the man had left pregnant with twins.
Brooke Timber is in need of a nanny, so what else can
Nick do but fill in? She's planning his father's wedding,
and all the family togetherness soon has Brooke and
Nick rethinking if this promise is still temporary...*

*Read on for a sneak preview of
A Promise for the Twins,
the next great book in Melissa Senate's
The Wyoming Multiples miniseries.*

If the Satler triplets were a definite, adding this client for July
would mean she could take off the first couple weeks of August,
which were always slow for Dream Weddings, and just be with
her twins.

Which would mean needing Nick Garroway as her nanny—
manny—until her regular nanny returned. Leanna could take some
time off herself and start mid-August. Win-win for everyone.

A temporary manny. A necessary temporary manny.

"Well, I've consulted with myself," Brooke said as she put
the phone on the table. "The job is yours. I'll only need help until
August 1. Then I'll take some time off, and Leanna, my regular
nanny, will be ready to come back to work for me."

He nodded. "Sounds good. Oh—and I know your ad called
for hours of nine to one during the week, but I'll make you a
deal. I'll be your around-the-clock nanny, as needed—for room
and board."

She swallowed. "You mean live here?"

"Temporarily. I'd rather not stay with my family. Besides, this way, you can work when you need to, not be boxed into someone else's hours."

Even a part-time nanny was very expensive—more than she could afford—but Brooke had always been grateful that necessity would make her limit her work so that she could spend real time with her babies. Now she'd have as-needed care for the twins without spending a penny.

Once again, she wondered where Nick Garroway had come from. He was like a miracle—and everything Brooke needed right now.

"I think I'm getting the better deal," she said. "But my grandmother always said not to look a gift horse in the mouth." Especially when that gift horse was clearly a workhorse.

"Good. You get what you need and I make good on that promise. Works for both of us."

She glanced at him. He might be gorgeous and sexy, and too capable with a diaper and a stack of dirty dishes, but he wasn't her fantasy in the flesh. He was here because he'd promised her babies' father he'd make sure she and the twins were all right. She had to stop thinking of him as a man—somehow, despite how attracted she was to him on a few different levels. He was her nanny, her *manny*.

But what was sexier than a man saying, "Take a break, I'll handle it. Take that call, I've got the kids. Go rest, I'll load the dishwasher and fold the laundry"?

Nothing was sexier. Which meant Brooke would have to be on guard 24/7.

Because her brain had caught up with her—the hot manny was moving into her house."

Don't miss
A Promise for the Twins *by Melissa Senate,*
available July 2019 wherever
Harlequin® Special Edition *books and ebooks are sold.*

www.Harlequin.com